Totally Bound Publishing books by Sara Ohlin

Graciella
Handling the Rancher
Seducing the Dragonfly
Flirting with Forever

Rescue Me
Salvaging Love
Igniting Love

Graciella

FLIRTING WITH FOREVER

SARA OHLIN

Flirting with Forever
ISBN # 978-1-83943-980-3
©Copyright Sara Ohin 2021
Cover Art by Erin Dameron-Hill ©Copyright May 2021
Interior text design by Claire Siemaszkiewicz
Totally Bound Publishing

FLIRTING WITH FOREVER

Dedication

To Izzy, my sister-in-law, my beautiful friend and the first person to ever read one of my manuscripts and encourage me to keep writing romance. A million thanks for all your support. I love you, lady!

Chapter One

It wasn't every day a man got to stand in the most perfect, spectacular place on earth. Lush farmland, rows of apple trees, green hills rolling off into the Pacific Ocean. A fantasy map drawn to perfection. Exactly what dreams were made of. Adam Brockman got to live it.

Gonna be another scorcher. Adam shielded his eyes from the blinding sun and took in the farm spread out below him. This land had never looked better. Full to bursting with things growing and thriving, crops, trees, animals, his family. The back of his pickup stood open and he shoveled farm compost, or good old-fashioned manure, whose ripe and humid scent wafted around him, beside the new walkways strewn throughout the farm.

First week of November and summer temperatures still beat relentlessly at the land. Long rays streaked across the colored leaves and toyed with the dirt drifting across the ground. But he wasn't fooled. Fall beckoned right around the corner, despite the heat.

With the trees exposing their reds and yellows and the sun sinking earlier, the land was preparing for hibernation. The knowledge tightened in his bones. It charged through him, the change in the air. But for a few more dreamy days he subscribed to the mirage. He would be perfectly fine if they had summer's sunshine and warmth all year long.

But damn, he hadn't planned on planting hundreds of perennials in ninety-degree heat. He'd already added tulip and daffodil bulbs. Come spring, the hard, monotonous work he'd put in would pay off, with gorgeous blooms lining the paths. Although Adam preferred working with the horses, beautifying his family farm was important to him, to all his brothers now. The threat of old ghosts was finally demolished, allowing them to make Brockman Farms shine again. They'd spent months cleaning her up, nurturing her. Lily was nearly finished with all the cottages. Yes, come spring this place would be brilliant.

"Shit!" Adam yelled as his puppy, Bullet, streaked by in a wisp of golden fur chasing something, probably imaginary, and tripping Adam in the process. He lost his footing on the slippery ground, his bucket and shovel flying from his hands, and found himself butt down in the pile of compost he'd just finished mounding over the sedum. Being surrounded by manure, as a farmer, was nothing new, but marinating in it wasn't on his agenda. "It's a good thing you're cute, you menace!" Christ, now the scent did more that waft around him, it oozed into his skin.

"What...what the hell?" A throaty, indignant voice interrupted his predicament. To his side stood a woman, bathed in the dusty glow of lazy sunlight, and compost. *Well, shit is right.* It was mostly at her feet, covering her shoes and ankles, and splattered on her jeans. A few globs clung to her cute T-shirt she had tied at her waist. Adam closed his eyes, banishing his clusterfuck, then risked peeking. There was even shit in her long hair, brown streaks of it splotched on her honey-blonde waves.

"You've got to be kidding me." She tried to stomp her foot, but with the wet pile of poop, her boot made more of a squelching sound. "Shit!"

Adam couldn't help the laugh that exploded out of him.

"This is not funny." Eyes narrowed, she skewered him with a look.

"It isn't?" Adam tried to keep the question out of his voice. He took in his body splayed in a pile of cow shit, raised his head and grinned at her. He couldn't tell from his spectacularly awkward spot on the ground if she wanted to scream at him or demand help. She'd just been assaulted with manure. Okay, okay, maybe it wasn't funny on her end.

Swallowing back his laughter, he said, "I'm so sorry, gorgeous." Dragging himself up, he tossed the shovel out of her way and offered his hand to help her out of her stuck situation.

"Gorgeous?" She huffed at him.

"Uh…" *She doesn't think she's gorgeous or she doesn't want me to tell her she's gorgeous?*

Deep chestnut eyes held more than disbelief or anger. Stories lingered there, buried deep. People always said so much more with their eyes than they realized. A smear of super-organic plain old manure stuck to her cheek. He reached for the bandana in his back pocket, then barely stopped himself from laughing again when he realized there was no way his compost-soaked cloth would do her any good now.

"A bit clumsy today, darlin'. I'd offer you my bandana" — Adam gestured to the disaster he now was — "but I'd get compost all over you, or *more* over you." He made to wipe his hands on his jeans, but he was covered in shit.

"Don't," she said and shoved her hands up.

"Look, you're stuck in…well, you don't want to stay there, do you?"

"It's cow poop! You *flung* it at me. I'm literally covered in shit. Why is it all over the place, anyway?" She reached up to pull a piece of hair away from her cheek. "Ugh!"

"I'm planting," Adam said. "Didn't expect my dog to toss me over. Or a beautiful stranger to come traipsing through and be caught in the shitstorm." He couldn't help it. His inner ten-year-old self found all the jokes and puns about this hilarious.

This hardened the indignant freeze in her eyes and shuttered all her hidden tales. Shame. He could wade in and happily discover each one.

"What is it with you people?" Wow, he was amazed at how angry she could make her words sound with her lips so tight and rigid. *Sure has pretty lips, though.*

"People?" He put his hands on his hips and got ready to face off with this gorgeous but prissy lady. He wasn't mad — it took a lot to anger him — but he did take pride in his work. Plus, if she wanted an argument, he was happy to provide one. Bantering with a pretty lady was much more fun than digging in the dirt.

"Men!"

She wiped the spot on her cheek but all it did was smear it across her flushed skin.

"Oh." Adam relaxed and smiled at her. "I thought it was farmers that ruffled your feathers. It's *men* you don't like."

"Yes, arrogant jerks with your swaggers and winks, tossing 'gorgeous' and 'darlin'' around thinking all women lap that up. And I do not have feathers! Ugh!"

Laughter bubbled out of him again. "You *do* know what a figure of speech is, though, right?" He checked his surroundings. *I'm still on the farm. Haven't stepped into an alternate dimension or anything.* "This is all my fault and I'm sincerely sorry. Here, please take my hand and step out of that mess."

"No...I..." She shooed his arm away. "This is unbelievable and yet so fitting at the same time."

Are we having two separate conversations? "Are you mad because of the sh—compost? Or because I like to use the correct words to address something? Do you not like people calling you gorgeous?"

"Ugh, men always thinking a woman's worth is only through her appearance."

"That's not what I said or meant. Don't go putting extra thoughts in my head."

She nodded and gave him a fake smile that did not match the rest of her expression. "Right. Of course. Is your head overloaded already?"

Points for sarcasm. Probably wise not to laugh this time. Oh yeah, she's ready to spar. It was entertaining watching her try to insult him. Adam's defenses were a steel vault. Her insults were nothing compared to what he and his brothers threw at each other. Even so, she still confused the hell out of him. "Why...go to all that trouble—" He swore as he rubbed the sweat off his forehead with the back of his hand. He probably had a nice streak of manure on his face now too.

"What was that?"

"*Now* you want to hear my thoughts?" he drawled as he peeled his work gloves off and tossed them aside.

"It's not polite to mumble at people."

"I *said*, why do women go to all the trouble in the world to appear gorgeous, with your sparkly makeup to highlight the gold flecks in your stunning eyes and hair products to entice seductively soft locks, but prance around like a snobby cat the minute we *dumb* men comment on it?" He intended to provoke her a bit, tangle her up, but damn he sank into the shimmering depths of her eyes.

"How I dress or wear makeup does not give you the right to hit on me. It's polite to address people by their names, not stereotypical monikers perpetuated by society's gender biases."

"Oh." Adam barked out a laugh. There was no sense trying to hide his humor, since she was zapping him left and right. "I wasn't hitting on you, but I get it now. You're giving the poor dumb farmer lessons in politesse." He stepped closer. *Dang! Prickly and stuck-up though she is, she sure smells pretty, like wildflowers in a sunny field*. It obliterated everything else, like a shot of adrenaline. He wanted to lie down in a meadow with her and explore her scent. They could argue and kiss and learn each other's bodies. *Whoa, slow down, slim.*

"Wha-what?" She blinked. "No—"

He didn't give her a chance to finish because what had started out as enjoyable banter had turned into a confusing tumbleweed blowing around inside him. *What is that feeling? Annoyance, frustration, agitation?* There was a whole lot of agitation going on in his chest and other places right now and he needed to get the heck away from her. But first he put his large hands on her waist, lifted her out of the shit pile and placed her gently back on the path that wasn't covered in manure.

"Oh," she gasped but placed her hands on his shoulders to steady herself, stretching her body closer to his.

Her touch annihilated any lingering lightheartedness of this situation. Instinct and manners warred in his body, heart and head, with instinct wanting him to tug her tight into his body. They'd fit in all the right places. His head ordered him to flee immediately. *Is that my head issuing orders?* His synapses were all jammed up. Her eyes fluttered closed and he wanted to shake her gently, make her open them back up when he kissed her.

WTF? Red warning lights flashed. He ripped his hands off her soft hips. "Sorry I ruined your boots, miss." He tipped his cowboy hat to her in one last stupid flourish and headed toward his north star, the barns. "Maybe stay away from us idiots," he yelled over his shoulder. "I guarantee you'll enjoy your stay better."

Chapter Two

"What? Wait!" Cass yelled to his surly manure-covered backside. She took in her new outfit now splattered with the same *eau du cow* and wanted to throw a mini hissy fit because if anything deserved a fit, it was being clobbered with cow poo. Instead she forced out some calming breaths. *Did all that really happen?* She glanced his way. He completely ignored her and disappeared down the hill, flinging his hands out in his own exasperating conversation. Yes. This was her reality. Right here. Right now.

One minute she'd been wandering through the perfect late morning on a gorgeous farm, breathing in the stillness, feeling a calming serenity she never enjoyed in the city and only melting a tiny bit under the obnoxious heat. The next minute a mini tornado of activity and yelling had whipped in front of her and she'd been assaulted with shit. One big pile of manure. Compost, he'd kept calling it, as if that made it better. He, giant of a man with a ridiculous smile on his face and his "I'm super charming" words. *Men! Idiot!*

Well, is there really much difference? Manure and compost? Man and buffoon? First with his cheesy swagger and charm, then stalking away all miffed. Apparently, men had vulnerable feathers too. Although she couldn't quite figure out why *he* was upset.

Maybe you confused him when your attitude switched to almost kissing him. She huffed at herself this time. *Hush. I merely leaned in to not fall when he lifted me.* Cass gingerly lifted her shirt away from her sweaty chest, dazed, like she'd been riding a bull and gotten tossed clean off.

Now the peacefulness settled back around her and she stood alone breathing *it* in everywhere—warm, humid, stinky cow poop. The universe had a remarkably unfunny sense of humor.

"You can't be a food writer if you can't smell the food, Cass." Truth smacked her in the face.

It's not only food, she'd wanted to cry to her editor last week. She hadn't smelled anything since that bleak day seventeen months ago. Nothing, not lilacs blooming in spring or freshly ground coffee beans or the way a summer rainstorm woke up the dry land. Hell, she might not even have known if her apartment had caught fire.

"I gave you a chance at the technology beat, but let's face it, your heart and style aren't there. Take a break. You need it."

A break? She'd been broken for what clawed at her like a million years. She was tired of being broken. She wiped her hands on her jeans and tried to fling off some of the offending mess while she headed back to her cottage.

What she *needed* was to put herself back together. She'd dug her car out of the garage two days ago and started driving from San Francisco. Leaving California behind had felt necessary in a way, a deep cleansing. Once she'd crossed the border into Oregon, she'd gotten off the main highway and meandered through the hills, windows down, taking ridiculous full, loud breaths and blowing out the collected dust of her depression, her sorrow, her disgust.

Brockman Farms had appeared as if it were a secret, enchanted place after a quick rainstorm, an intriguing beauty on the coast of Oregon. The gorgeous hand-painted sign and the notice of coastal cottages to rent had drawn her in.

Her sister-in-law had been urging her to go away on some tropical all-inclusive vacation where she could relax, meet hot men, maybe have an affair and be served cocktails while sitting poolside.

The last thing on Cass' agenda was more cocktails or men. Annabelle thought Cass was still mourning. 'Mourn' wasn't the right word anymore. Oh, she'd sunk into its quicksand hold the first year, but then her body had begun shedding its numbness, leaving her restless and angry. For the past few months, she'd been stupid in her pursuit to feel *anything*.

It was past time to get her life back on a healthy path. No more stupid decisions while drinking, no more burying her head in the sand to hide her tears.

"Oh! Wow! Are you okay? Did you fall? Oh my gosh."

People materialize out of the golden air around here.

"I'm Lily. I'm finishing up renovations on the last cottage. You're staying in Kilrush? Our first guest. We're all so excited, but..." The woman took a breath, waved her hand around Cass and finished, "That is not the welcome we'd planned. What happened?"

A stallion kicked poop at me. Calm down — now you're the one comparing him to an animal. "One of the farmers, I

16

think, lost control of his dog and his shovel full of manure."

Lily burst out laughing. "You're joking! Oh! I'm so sorry. I know it's not funny except I can picture Adam and his dog. It had to be Adam. He's the kindest, gentlest most well-mannered one of them. Did he turn bright red from embarrassment?" The woman's infectious spirit deflated Cass' pissy mood. It *was* funny. Kind of. And no, he had not been the least bit embarrassed. At least not until he'd touched her.

"There are more of them?"

Lily's smile widened. She stood with her hands on her hips and her legs spread like a pixie-sized goddess on top of the world. Her shirt and overalls were a mess, but underneath all the dirt and dust, she exuded power and confidence, her face bright and happy. "Three Brockman Brothers. Cruz, Turner and Adam."

"Are they all so clumsy?"

Lily wiped tears of laughter. "Not usually. Wait till I tell Turner." She smacked her forehead. "Annnd I should be helping you. Sorry, a little socially awkward sometimes."

"It's okay. You made me see the humor in it." *Among other realizations.* Cass had truly believed her sense of smell had vanished for good, until this ridiculous moment. *Or fifteen surreal moments before.*

Of course *shit* would resurrect her senses.

But it was more. Cass could smell *everything.* A singularly unique perfume surrounded them, a dry end-of-fall heat, musty flowers and plant life. A brininess hinted in the air. And she could smell it all — stinky, warm farm life shining in all its glory before winter came in with her graceful death. She leaned her face up to the sun and bathed in it, quietly breathing in the dry land, the farm's essence drifting around her.

"Beautiful, isn't it?" Serene now, Lily's gaze followed Cass'.

A view of the dark Pacific, still like glass today, stretched to the west and in front of them — the website had it correct — one breathtaking gem of a place. All deep-green hills, empty dirt rows where crops had been harvested, funny looking Brussels sprouts and potato plants lined up. More rows of apple trees, their branches almost bare now. Even the requisite red barns glowing in the valley and surrounded by a bright blue sky. The paths strewn throughout had called to her. A charming secret town.

"Mmm. I'm Cassandra, Cass, by the way. I promise not to shake hands." The manure had dried, leaving a cracked brown pattern on her fingers. "Do you live here?"

"Turner and I live up the cliffs, away from the farm by about ten minutes. I've traveled all over, but this still takes my breath away every day."

"It reminds me of a fairy tale."

"Don't let Adam hear you say that. He'll propose on the spot." Lily chuckled.

Cass' smile faltered. She tried to hide the flinch.

"Gosh, forgive me. I'm kidding," Lily said. "I have a habit of blurting things out. Don't mind me."

"It's okay. I think I'll head back now. Hopefully that gorgeous walk-in shower in the master bath can wage war on this stink."

"That shower was fun to design. I do apologize for the buffoon. The brothers are genuinely nice guys, Adam especially. I hope the rest of your stay is uneventful. Let us know if you need anything." Lily headed toward the large main house.

Brockman House.

The brochures in her cottage detailed the renovations and plans for a café due to open in the next few months. She'd read about it a few weeks ago too in a *Travel Oregon* magazine at the dentist's office. It seemed too good to be true, but when she'd decided to get away from the city, away from any hovering judgments or connections to anyone, this gorgeous setting and business on the cusp of blossoming into the rustic, back-to-earth food scene had called to Cass. Her heart had trilled with hope. If she really could smell again, maybe she'd find a way back into the culinary writing world and save her career.

Not just any career. Cass wound her way back to the cottage. Her *dream*. Writing about food and restaurants for one of the major newspapers in the country. A position she'd carved out of stone to excel at above all others. And she had, until her world had crumbled beneath her.

Kicking off her cute suede booties by the front door, Cass pouted at the loss of them. They'd end their life drunk on compost. "Stinky, pretty shoe ruiner."

At first, after her husband's death, when she'd lost her sense of smell, she hadn't even noticed. It wasn't until her first assignment back to work reviewing the newest Asian fusion restaurant in Nobb Hill when, in bringing a bowl of spicy ramen to her nose, she'd realized she couldn't smell a thing. Then she'd been too depressed to care.

But her sense of smell barreling back in right now was confusing. Part of her wanted to be dancing circles of celebrational glee. At the same time, it left her aching as memories of all she'd lost washed over her. Some scents she'd never be able to reclaim. The smell of Nathan's neck when she'd leaned in to hug him. The way paint and varnish had lingered on his hands after a day teaching art. The best roast chicken he'd made specially for her.

Will grief ever let me go? There were moments it played like a broken record, forcing her to relive her pain, over and over.

My socks are squishy. Eventually, real life always charged back in. Cass peeled off the offending socks. *Gross!*

I cannot believe I got hit with mid-air manure by a farmer. For idiots' sake, she'd been surrounded by enough testosterone assholes in the newsroom and in restaurants. Cass chewed on her lip — then immediately stopped because who knew where else the manure had landed on her face and the last thing she needed was to eat some.

Although, while his muscles and his large hands had screamed testosterone, his demeanor had been kind and silly. He'd used the word *gorgeous* like it had been bred into his manners, not as a cheesy way of insulting her. And she hadn't been kind or forgiving. Good Lord, she'd lost all tact with human interactions. Exhaustion and sweltering heat had made her cranky and snippy.

"Stunning eyes." The man could fluster Eeyore. Had anyone noticed her eyes in forever?

When he'd lifted her, an invitation apparently for her hands to reach out and grasp his warm, powerful shoulders, He hadn't been intrusive or rude as she'd expected. He'd been gentlemanly, if she had to give it an old-fashioned term.

Until he'd cast his attitude.

He'd drawled out his words, but what she'd noticed was how deep his voice had gotten. *Almost angry-sounding and husky.* It was all mixed up in her head because as soon as he'd gotten close, *her* anger had disappeared and she'd leaned into him.

Mmm-hmm. Told you.

Hush! I haven't kissed anyone since Nathan. I'm not kissing anyone.

She shed her clothes and let the water heat to steaming. *Adam.* She'd wanted to explore his dark lashes that hinted at warm, smoky seduction. But she'd closed her eyes and swooned like a fool instead. Even through the humid manure his scent had provoked her, warm hay, spice and sweat. Cass tried to call back that tiny moment of curiosity and desire that had engulfed her.

Boy, do I need a shower.

As she allowed the gorgeous rain showerhead and superb water pressure to take away her stress, Cass selected an amazing lemongrass body wash and finally did her own tiny dance of glee while she luxuriated in scents returning to her. The water opened her senses further and she let herself imagine. It was only moments until she found herself in a breathtaking daydream surrounded by a hot man with frustration in his grip who smelled like things primal...scents that aroused and mesmerized and turned a cleansing shower steamy.

Chapter Three

"Great! Let's recap. Don't spray a woman with manure. Don't offer to help her get unstuck from that manure. And especially don't act like the backend of an orangutan and call her gorgeous." Adam reprimanded himself as the overheated, dusty barn air flitted around him like annoying bees, blowing in his face one minute and gone the next.

"Talking to yourself again?" his brother Cruz called out from feeding the cows.

"Yep."

"You plant all those perennials?"

"Nope."

Cruz looked up the hill toward Adam's pickup. "Did you forget something?"

"Yep." *My brain. Or my heart. My heart-brain?*

"You all right?"

"Yep." *Nope.*

"Alrighty then. Good talk." Cruz smacked his shoulder and left him in the middle of the dairy barn. People worked seamlessly around him. Voices echoed.

Someone laughed. Huge steel machines hummed. Hay and warm milk and cows seeped into his conscience. It settled him, the business, the routine, the simple order of things he recognized, barn and animal scents, old beams, his brother's voice.

How did that go so spectacularly wrong?

The hustle at this time of morning was exactly what he needed to ground himself back on the planet. Had he left his truck and his task of planting a gazillion flowers and shrubs behind? *Yep.* Had he behaved kind of like an idiot? No *kind of* about it. Was he mentally smacking himself upside the head? Sure was. *Good, glad we got that covered.*

Unprecedented. He closed his eyes and winced as the scene replayed in his head. He'd executed a poop attack. *Unprecedented? More like moronic.* When things had settled and reality had hit his eyes and his nose, it had been instinctual to laugh with her over it, which had earned him one snooty glare. She sure was cute all pissed off.

Their verbal battle was no less amusing. Until he'd gotten close. Until his brain had been short-circuited by her scent. Until her fingers had touched his shoulders and he'd taken a punch.

Hard.

Right. In. The. Chest. Direct hit.

And he'd acted like a charming fucking asshole.

So, he'd take a moment, right here in his safe place. Beg his breath to come the fuck back. Talk himself down from whatever cliff of insanity he'd been shoved to.

He wanted to turn around and gaze at her. Wanted to go right back up the hill, keep his mouth shut and act like he *wasn't* the dumbest man on the planet. *I thought women liked compliments.* Adam shook his head, trying to clear the residue of confusion. Apparently, he was rustier than he'd imagined—a corroded engine. He hadn't meant to say *gorgeous* out loud, even though it had been railroading through his mind.

But he didn't turn around and he did not go back up the hill to make a bigger ass of himself. He stayed put until the dizzying sensation left his body, and until he knew he wouldn't trip up figuratively or literally. *No sense getting zapped further by her sharp tongue.* Even if it was surrounded by the prettiest, lushest mouth he'd ever seen. No, he didn't turn around to get chastised *or* fall in deep to her eyes full of stories. He waited it out, breathing, calming his racing heartbeat. He could stand here all day. His brothers didn't call him a stubborn bull for no reason.

But when Adam finally had his body and emotions under control and headed back to his task, he let out the hopeful sigh he'd been holding onto, and his heart sank. She was no longer in sight.

* * * *

"Your turn, girl," Adam said. He tossed the ripe apple and walked toward the far secluded paddock in the quiet evening, dry and crisp from the sea breeze. The sun, setting earlier each day, snuck her rays through the trees, casting fairy dances across the ground. "I know you want more play time, but it's going to be dark soon, sugar." His horse Gracie twirled her head at him and stomped her hooves in the dirt. If a horse could act snooty, Gracie had it down pat. And she was all the more amazing for it.

Adam smiled. They were all his horses now, all twelve of them. As of yesterday, the new agreement had been signed. Now he and his brothers were equal owners of all two hundred and fifty thousand acres. But they'd put the horses solely in his name. Truly, they were all he ever wanted.

Well, the horses and a piece of Brockman land to finally build his own home. He could pick anywhere on the farm now. For years, ideas and house plans had lived in his dreams. He couldn't wait to make them a reality.

"You're the one who truly belongs here," Cruz had said when they'd learned all those months ago that through his will, T.D. Brockman had screwed his youngest son, Adam, by leaving him nothing. T.D. had tried to screw all three of his sons, but he'd failed spectacularly. They'd been far more intelligent and cunning than T.D. could have known, but they also had something their father had lacked. Love for the land, love for each other. Together, as a family, they were rebuilding Brockman Farms.

Cruz was partly correct, or had been. Adam did belong to the land and the land to him. He'd always been connected to this sacred ground. But now his brothers were too, and by choice, by love.

"I know you think if you pretend to ignore me, I won't put you in the barns, but that won't work." He climbed through the rails and walked over to the massive black mare waiting for him. Healthy now, she stood proud at over six feet. Her mane gleamed and shimmered, and her eyes smiled, no longer haunted.

The horses had always been his love, his passion, his friends. Even when his father, T.D., had been alive and had tried to make Adam understand that in order to get a horse to submit and obey, they had to be beaten.

Now T.D. was dead. *Best ten months of my life so far.* His family was back together and expanding. Cruz was newly married to Miranda. Turner and Lily were engaged. The barns were repaired. Updated equipment had been installed. New horses were being born, and Adam got to be in the center of it all, in fact, covered by it, if the state of his jeans and work shirt were any indication. He was a walking add for a pigsty, and he smelled like one too.

"Here, sugar. Brought you a treat." He saved Gracie's goodnight for last every day so they could talk. He and his girl. Shit, it was a good thing his brothers couldn't hear his ridiculous thoughts. They'd never cease making fun of him. Even though he was twenty-seven and bigger physically than Cruz and Turner, they still teased him as if he were the scrawny, freckled little brother when it came to women. Good thing he could tease them right back. They'd both turned into love-struck yahoos when it came to their fiancées.

Adam hadn't dated often. Cruz hilariously hinted maybe he should try new with new conversation topics that had nothing to do with unique equine knowledge or farming, but Adam simply hadn't connected with anyone. He was waiting for his perfect woman. She'd be there when he was ready, in a year or two. Once he'd built his house. He knew exactly what he wanted in a wife. Someone younger, beautiful, wide-eyed. Someone who loved the farm as much as he did. Someone to make a family with. He wanted the chance to be a better father to his own sons than T.D. had been.

Turner had shed tears of hilarity at his checklist, but Adam thought it dumb *not* to make a list of things he desired in a wife. Aside from this farm, getting married was one of the most important things he planned to do in life. He'd find her when he was ready. They'd click right away. And his life would be complete.

Ah, hell. Is the joke on me?

He certainly hadn't expected to splatter her with poop as a way of introduction, or for his heart to beat out of his chest at the sight of her. They'd absolutely *not* clicked this morning. Her temper had hushed his crazy skyrocketing emotions, which was a good thing because he'd been able to wipe away his drool without her noticing.

Then she'd taken offense to everything he uttered, and in turn, he'd acted as stinky as the manure she was stuck in. He'd have to ask Lily and Miranda how he'd tangled himself up so absurdly.

"Atta girl, beautiful. There you go." He held his palm open with the apple for her to grasp. "Now eat up. It's time to go in for the night. *You* don't mind when I give you pretty compliments." He should have stuck with the horses this morning, stayed safe in the barn where he couldn't bean anyone with poop bombs. Adam grabbed Gracie's lead and tried to head them both toward the barn, but she wouldn't budge.

Gazing in the direction his intelligent horse aimed her focus, he saw the woman from this morning standing on her cottage's front porch, leaning against the railing. Had his dreams conjured her? Adam couldn't peel his eyes away. She'd invaded his mind all day. How indignant she'd been, how stupid *he'd* been.

He had eventually gotten the perennials planted, waiting, hoping she'd reappear and they could start over.

God, she *was* pretty. Nearly as tall as Adam with long, straight honey-colored hair and hips for days.

He'd had his hands on those hips. Had wanted to drag her into him. Her hair had fluttered around them in the breeze. It was her huge brown eyes he'd gotten lost in. His casual and friendly demeanor had gone up in flames when he held her. She'd given him one quick, chance view into her soul and his heart wanted to understand all of her. Before she'd shied her secrets away, closed her eyes and sighed into him.

Now you're getting carried away again.

Gracie tossed her head, whinnied and gave a little dance in the woman's direction. "Show off. How come you got the smooth moves?" He cast his gaze between them. *There's her smile.* It snared his heart and flung it into the sky. Adam raised his hand. Was it in greeting? In apology? Perhaps truce? *Feels more like recognition.*

She mimicked him, gave a small smile then ducked inside.

Adam stood watching, wondering if he could lasso his heart back into his chest, or if he even wanted to.

Chapter Four

Oh my God! I'm an idiot. Cass tried to make her dash inside more subtle than ogling the man and his horse with complete abandon. *Adam.* She knew his name now. *The same man whose hands still brand my waist, warm, strong, electric.*

She'd been sitting on the front porch, eyes closed, trying not to sink into the complete exhaustion that had washed over her body pretty much since she'd arrived here. It had been for longer, truthfully, but was intensified here. The magical air surrounding this place cast a sleeping spell upon her.

His voice had conjured her attention. Deep and carefree, strong, without a hint of frustration in it. *Surely he's talking to himself, because no one else is around.* But when she'd peeked, he'd been crooning to the horse. *How silly.* Although, who wouldn't want to whisper sweet nothings to that stunning mare? The lady held herself regal and proud, practically commanding the audience to adore her.

Cass observed through the opening in the curtain. Such a contrast they were, man and beast. The magnificent midnight horse, all thriving energy and piercing black eyes. What would she feel like under Cass flying across the land? *She's full of mysteries and desires.* Dark to the man's light. The giant mare teased and frolicked next to her human. *Ahh, she has a sense of humor too.*

The man was no less magnificent. Also huge with his own gorgeous muscles, he had a relaxed, almost lazy grace to his movements. Teasing the horse with treats and that soothing voice. They created their own unique dance and communicated without words. The horse flirted with him and he laughed and feinted and indulged her for a while until the beauty finally sauntered right up next to him to have her forehead rubbed.

Cass closed her eyes and dreamed. *Mmm, what that caress must do to a body. What I wouldn't give to have him soothe my head, my worries.* With his hat off, his wavy red hair curled against his skin. Perhaps his eyes were a deep brown. His cheeks had flushed, highlighting his freckles this morning when she'd been chastising him. The true nature of his eyes might have eluded her, but not his full lips though. Oh no, she didn't even have to close her eyes to picture his mouth. Thick and full and waiting to be kissed.

And she nearly had kissed him. Images of riding and longing soared through her mind, and she wondered what *he* would feel like spread out under her. *Bet that ride might kill a person. Death by sexual bliss.* Cass nearly crumpled at the luscious, erotic thoughts.

Gah! She rubbed her dry, tired eyes. *Quit imagining the man naked.* What a mess. *Is there something wrong with me?* She'd survived, dammit! She'd kept her shit together, *mostly*, for the last year and a half. Made it past the worst parts. But there was no map of what to do now that the lockdown on her emotions had burst. She'd been a different kind of mess the last few months since she'd longed for sensation again, for any touch or emotion aside from numb.

Now being here amongst all this beauty, draining fatigue dogged her every day. This morning, scents had surged back in, and a nasty side of her personality had lashed out. She'd heard about people who kept it together through stressful situations then, when their bodies somehow knew it was okay to relax, or when the damn burst, the stress seeped out like puss from a wound. *Is that what this trip suggests to my body? That it's time to purge?*

The swaggering, muscly cowboy had played with his beautiful horse as the sun had set. Cass had watched the evening curl around them and had wanted to be a part of their tiny circle of warmth and love. Finally, he'd walked her gently away, the horse nudging his face, teasing him, comforting him too. He'd given one lingering glance back toward Cass' cottage, then disappeared across the hill. *Don't go. Let me entertain my curiosity from behind the curtain. At a safe distance.*

His wave had been kind. At least from here, she could make herself believe he wasn't still angry. Had he really been mad this morning? Maybe he had a teeny, tiny right to be after the way she'd spoken to him, but Cass wasn't so sure it was anger that burned from him. *Lust,* hummed through her brain in answer. The absurdity of that almost mad her laugh, but the next question clear in her mind was, *his or mine?*

Treating people to her snotty side was not her norm. What had come over her earlier? It had had nothing to do with his darlins' and calling her gorgeous. It had to do with such fucking aching loneliness inside her that she was no longer able to mask. Everyone had a breaking point. Apparently hers was manure.

In another lifetime, she'd have laughed along with him. It *was* funny, flying manure. Crappy *and* funny. She was like that gorgeous mare, pent-up, restless. Would he soothe her the way he did his horse? Cass could certainly add *confused* to her own emotions. When he'd touched her, her body had longed for his and his alone. *How can such a thing even be?*

Her head pounded again — or, more like, continued its rage. It hadn't stopped since she'd woken this morning. *Maybe I'm sick too, in addition to a full mental purge? Sure, why not toss a little icing onto the cake.* Without putting up much of a fight, she folded her body onto the oversized couch for nap number two of the day and replayed her encounter with Adam.

Are people really that direct and corny at the same time? Perhaps it was Cass who was the dork for taking offense. Polite and chivalrous were indeed outdated. His hands on her certainly weren't corny. His proud jaw and what she could only imagine were strong enormous thighs. *Ahh, I bet he's enormous everywhere.* In her state of flattened tired, she smiled at images of him before she sank into a deep sleep.

* * * *

Cass came awake weighted and groggy. The spins attacked her head and she tried to hush them by sitting up. When she stood, her stomach lurched. With a start, she rushed into the bathroom. A cold sweat broke out over her skin, but she heaved absolutely nothing up. Nothing because she hadn't eaten in almost two days. Or longer, she couldn't remember. It was her normal since grief had kidnapped her ability to smell and taste. When she did eat, it was more because she felt hunger, not desire. It was rote and necessary. There hadn't been much enjoyment in food when it all smelled bland and boring. It almost made her smile to think of all the things she'd relish eating now that scent and aroma belonged to her again. But even a smile was too much exercise at the moment when every move made her entire body ache.

Well damn. So much for relaxing or rejuvenating. If her body had decided to let out all her caged stress from the last year and a half, this was only the beginning. She had a shit-ton of crap built up. *Ha, shit-ton. It's following me everywhere.* Cass rested her forehead on the edge of the cold tub. It sucked being sick when she was alone. She didn't even know if she was capable of getting up. She reached to push her tired body off the floor, but her arms gave out.

Nope, no energy. I'll just stay here for a bit. Cass tugged the hand towel down, wet it under the bath faucet and placed it on her clammy forehead, grateful for the cool bathroom surface and the lavender-scented softness of the towel.

"I know there are solitary people who don't mind being alone, but I'm not one of them." Cass' voice echoed in the empty bathroom. There were times when talking to herself had helped, but tonight wasn't one of them. Loneliness was an ache she couldn't escape from, no matter where she went.

Chapter Five

"It's a miracle! He's here, everyone." Adam's brother Turner slapped him on the back as he and Bullet walked into the kitchen at Brockman House. "You ever learn how to tell time?" Turner teased. Food filled the countertops, fixings for tacos, grilled veggies, chocolate cheesecakes.

"Adam." A chorus of different voices greeted him. Bullet raced out of the back door to tangle with the other dogs and a group of kids. Some belonged to Miguel and Roxanna, others to employees living on their property, and all of them were family in one way or another. Outdoor lights and heaters lit up the chilly evening.

Adam grabbed his brother in a bear hug. "You're hilarious. Do you just stand there and look pretty all day? Some of us have real work to do."

Cuban jazz came from the radio and amazing aromas hit him in the face, chilis and garlic and roasted onions. *Mmm*, his empty stomach cheered. Katie, Javier and Roxanna worked in the kitchen, putting the finishing touches on the meal. Cruz manned the bar, making cocktails and mocktails for the kids. Miguel and some friends stood out by the firepit, their faces glowing red from the flames.

These Sunday night gatherings had become tradition. In two weeks, they'd have their first barn dinner party in practice for the large outdoor dinners they wanted to have at the farm for locals in Graciella and anyone else, hopefully lots of others, visiting this part of the country. The first one would honor the brothers becoming the three legal owners of the farm. *A celebration. A triumph.*

"Work? Or play with the animals?" Turner asked.

"Luckily for me it's the same thing." Adam smiled and put his arm around Turner's fiancée, Lily. "You're much prettier than he is."

"Hands off, little brother. Find your own woman." Turner tugged Lily out from Adam's hug and gazed down at her.

Lily snuggled into Turner's body and returned his adoration. "You do know I'm not a piece of property."

"Too bad," Turner said, more quietly now as if he was speaking only to Lily, holding and swaying with her. "Because I've got you and I'm never letting go."

I can't wait to find that for myself.

A woman who, even surrounded by people and noise, would smile at him the way Lily smiled at Turner, as though her world had started when he came into her life. He wanted it all, love, marriage, kids, dogs and all the mess that came with it. Hope filled his chest.

"Adam." Lily interrupted his thoughts. "Heard you had a crappy morning." She dissolved into giggles before she could continue. *Guess poop humor stands the test of time.* An image of sparkling mad brown eyes lit with fire hit his mind. *Well, not everyone finds it funny.*

"You live to embarrass me, don't you?" Adam said.

"Oh," Lily continued through her laughter, "I think you embarrassed yourself spectacularly."

"What did he do?" His hand linked with Miranda's, Cruz walked up and handed Adam a beer.

"He threw manure all over the guest in Kilrush. Cass is her name. Poor thing."

Cass, pretty name for a pretty lady.

"I didn't throw it. Bullet had an attack of crazy and tripped me. I tossed my shovel, ended up in compost and flung it everywhere. She unfortunately got caught in the crossfire. You had to tell everyone, huh?" He elbowed Lily.

"Oh, honey, this is the best story ever!"

"Holy shit!" Cruz busted out laughing.

"Crap, you didn't?" Miranda gasped.

"All right, get all your jabs in now." Adam held up his hands. "I can take it. *She* wasn't amused. Can't blame her really. I ruined her boots and possibly her jeans. And I got it in her hair."

Miranda had a look of horror on her face.

"Did you apologize?" Turner asked.

"Of course, idiot, but she wasn't too keen on that either. She was all prickly and snobby."

"And beautiful," Lily said.

"Yeah," he sighed.

Lily smirked.

Shit! "Walked right into that one, didn't I?"

"Uh-oh." Cruz could barely talk through his laughter. "Do you need lessons on how to make a good first impression with the ladies?"

"Please, Cruz." Miranda laughed. "Did you forget your first impression on me, hanging up on me, calling me stuck up?"

Cruz put his arm around her. "You were gaga over me from that first moment."

Miranda smiled. "I went gaga when you shared your strawberry ice cream with me, that's for sure."

"Hey." Lily took pity on him. "When I talked to her, she didn't seem upset. She laughed about it. We chatted. And aside from the manure on her, she was entranced by this place."

"Take her some food as a peace offering," Miranda suggested.

"Food always works." Lily gave Turner a wink.

"Jesus, all of you are a bunch of fools in love," Adam said. He left them and followed the scent of grilled onions. "But you might be onto something," he tossed over his shoulder.

Despite their morning mix-up and mutual tongue lashing, he'd felt her pull, the lure of getting to know her, *Cass*, throughout the day. And when he'd caught her watching him and Gracie, leaning against her porch railing, silhouetted in the fading daylight, that pull had tightened in his gut. He'd snuck one last glance before he and Gracie had disappeared, and even though she'd already gone inside, he'd smiled and told his horse all about her soulful brown eyes.

Adam had always gone with his gut. And right now, it said, "*Go talk to her, see if your heart flips over like it did this morning.*"

"Mom." He came behind the island and gave her a hug. "I think I'm going to take mine to go tonight."

"Everything okay?" she asked.

It wasn't unusual for Adam to race in during their dinners, grab a bite and get back to work on the farm, especially during the long daylight hours of summer. *Ahh, I miss summer already.*

"Yeah, met the guest at Kilrush Cottage this afternoon." Maybe he wouldn't detail exactly how.

"Mmm-hmm." Katie went back to filling a bowl with fresh guacamole. He also never had to explain much to his mother. She'd always said he wore his emotions out in the open for everyone to see. He hadn't bothered changing and even T.D. hadn't been able to beat it out of him. "Going to take her dinner? Sounds lovely, but did you take into account whether she wants company or not?"

"She looked…" *Sad, beautiful.* "Intriguing."

"Don't forget alone," his mother warned with a soft hand on his arm. "Just because we all know what a big softy you are doesn't mean a stranger does, especially a woman by herself. And she might not want company. Not all our guests are going to want to join in the craziness."

"I kind of owe her an apology."

"Oh no, what did you do?"

"You don't want to know, trust me. Don't worry, I'll take her a plate of food. The aroma of your chicken soft tacos will warm anyone's heart. If she doesn't want to talk, at least she'll eat well."

He left out through the back, said a few quick greetings, whistled for Bullet and leashed his fluffy, newly bathed menace. After all, man and dog both owed her an apology. The leash was a must in case Bullet took off toward the beach, his favorite spot, or in case he got it in his head to stir up the dirt again. The goofball functioned at super speed or crashed out asleep these days. There was no in-between.

"Come on, buddy. I need you on your best behavior. Let's try to make a better second impression." Adam tightened his hold on the leash and carried the casserole dish full of fixings for chicken soft tacos. He'd tucked two beers in his jacket pocket.

They made it to her door in one piece with the food still intact and Bullet tried extra hard to behave as he sat on his butt and let out a tiny bark. Adam knocked. Soft light filtered through the windows and the door was ajar. *That's odd.*

"Hello, are you here?" Adam knocked again and his eyes caught sight of her legs on the bathroom floor. His instinct took over and he tugged on the leash. "Bullet, come!"

"Jesus Christ!" His stomach dropped. Cass lay slumped on the bathroom floor, out cold.

Chapter Six

Can I feel pain in my dreams? Cass' head throbbed. In fact, her entire body ached from something that must be the flu. *Maybe a truck ran over me.* She couldn't be awake. A nightmare maybe? *I'm so confused. Where am I?* Along with the pain, there were fuzzy moments of noises and voices. Was that knocking? And a clear, deep "Hello." *Who is Bullet?*

Boulders rested on her eyes. No matter how hard she tried, they wouldn't open. It really was like being in one of those weird never-ending dreams, always running, unable to reach the destination. Cass preferred the blackness of a dreamless sleep, a sleep she cherished. That was one more thing she wondered if she'd ever recover.

If she could just open her eyes... "Oh! What is going—" she cried out, her voice thin. Something warm and wet slapped at her face and she brought her hands up to shield herself, but her fingers met soft fur. Fur that was wiggling and moving and climbing on her.

Cass dragged her eyes open, hoping to get the hell out of whatever crazy dream she was in.

"Bullet, no! Bullet! I'm so sorry. Are you all right?"

Cass' body jerked and she tried to sit up, but her weak body slipped right down to the floor again. Warm hands held under her arms and lifted her so she was sitting, her back against the tub. "Steady?" Adam asked as he searched her eyes.

"I think," she said. "Am I awake?" *What are you doing here* almost poured out, but apparently her mouth wasn't communicating properly. Either that or his eyes had hypnotized her. *A dark sky blue.* She'd been wrong earlier—not a trace of brown. *I wonder if they ebb and flow through different hues, ocean waves.*

"You are."

If she was hypnotized by his eyes, it was his smile that pierced her, that dragged her right back to an intense reality. Cass swore her ribs expanded to make room for her broken heart.

"We didn't mean to startle you. Your door was open, and I thought you might be hurt. I'm Adam Brockman, one of the owners."

"We?" she said.

He smiled again and this time it completely muddled her mind.

"Bullet and me. He's…whoops, sorry, Bullet, no! Off!"

At the sound of his name, a mess of moving fur launched, plopped his butt down on the floor and started peppering her face with slobbery kisses. It seemed he wasn't too concerned with commands. Adam went to grab his collar, but Cass closed her arms around the large puppy and cuddled him closer. He was so warm and soft and she was freezing. "How

41

beautiful," she whispered. Apparently, the dog agreed because he gave a quick yip, fell onto her lap and rolled belly up, unabashedly begging for some loving.

Adam's smile relaxed. There was more warmth and ease. It held a secret. A good one? She couldn't discern.

"He's shy, in case you hadn't noticed." Now his smile was playful. Lord how many smiles did this man have? A lethal arsenal of them, zapping her one moment, luring her into fantasyland the next. "This klutz is Bullet." Adam reached over and unleashed him. "He aided and abetted in our debacle this morning."

"Oh," was all she could say. With her still groggy, his words swam through her head. But achy and unsure of herself sitting on the bathroom floor as she was, this man's presence, along with his dog, comforted her. "I saw you," she blurted out as if she were trying to make sense of things. "With your horse."

He nodded. "Gracie. Are you a horse whisperer of some kind? I couldn't beg her attention away even with the promise of sugar until you went inside. Do you like horses?"

"I love horses," she said. "Horses were summers on my grandmother's farm. I haven't ridden in years, though."

"And dogs." He encouraged her to keep talking. She looked back down at Bullet, his eyes half closed in puppy ecstasy as she rubbed his tummy. "And they like you," Adam observed. "I don't want to frighten you, but I could help you up if you like. Maybe get you more comfortable on the couch. I promise not to call you gorgeous or tease you with any annoying 'darlin's'."

A mix between a frown and a pout was almost sexier than his full-on smile. And the soothing cadence of his voice eased her confusion. "I brought food. We all get together on Sunday nights at the main house for dinner...I didn't mean to act like a complete jackass during the poop escapade, and when I saw you again—"

"Is that what you're calling it?" she asked and gave him a small teasing smile.

"I am so sorry about all of that," he said. He held one of her hands and rubbed her fingers through his. She was startled for a minute, their hands entwined.

"I was a bit snobby this morning."

"You had good reason. Maybe a good meal could be my apology?"

"I'm starving," she said and sounded surprised at her own admission. And the honesty kept flowing. "I haven't been hungry in weeks." *Years.*

His grin reached his eyes, which just about did her in. *Don't faint again. Don't faint again.*

Cass realized where she was sitting and her face heated with embarrassment. She was indeed sprawled across the tile with a wet washcloth stuck to her shoulder, her hair plastered to her forehead, a strange man and dog keeping her company. Still weak, she was grateful for his patience and calm.

"Come on, Bullet." He grabbed the dog's collar and led him out of the bathroom where he ordered him to sit and stay. *Huh, Cutie-pie is learning.* Then he bent down on one knee and asked, "Want some help?" He held his hands out.

Now there was no playful dog between them and he looked so intense. His smile was gone, but his face still held warmth. He was letting her call the shots. Did she want his help? Normally she didn't want anyone's.

But she didn't know if she could stand on her own, all her energy had disappeared leaving her floppy and uncertain. A groggy grasp on reality swam in her head.

It might be irrational of her to assume without really knowing him, but his nature and kindness felt genuine. It was the way he was with his animals, kind, honest, silly, loving. The people she'd met in life who treated animals with kindness and love had good hearts.

"I think I could use some assistance," she said.

He tilted his head a bit in question. "You sound upset with the admission. I'm okay leaving you alone. But I don't want you to faint again...is that what happened?"

"I think...I was nauseous and sweaty. I made it in here, got a washcloth, then the next thing I remember is Bullet's kisses waking me up." Cass still made no move to stand as she continued studying Adam. He was young, but confidence rested in his strong jaw and a few wrinkles around his eyes. Those blue pools rippled between the color of the sky and the sea. A lazy wave twinkling under the sun. Exactly like the man, lazy, uncomplicated, completely certain of his path.

"We could sit here and talk for a while until you're ready?" he offered. She tried to laugh, but just as quickly tears gathered in her eyes. How ridiculous that her most meaningful conversation in months was with a strange man and his dog on the bathroom floor because she was too weak to move. Could he see how wrung out, how empty she was? God, she couldn't even control her tears lately. Everything made her cry all the sudden, even more so than after Nathan's death. The sunset over the water, the smell of firewood burning in the evening mist, the charming cottage that was all hers to rent for as long as she wanted. Quietly

Bullet was there again in her lap, cleaning her tears with his tongue.

"His ability to stay needs work," Adam said. "If you'd prefer, I could call my mother or my sister-in-law to come help you. They could be over in a few minutes. My mother, Katie, would have been the one to let you into the cottage. Or Lily, you met her."

"I did." She nodded and wiped her face. "Today after our...well, after you and I met." The image of Lily doubled over in laughter made her grin. "She thought it was hilarious."

"Yeah, I got an earful from her and my brothers. Funniest thing they've heard in years." He exaggerated his words in mock annoyance, but his smile was gentle.

"Mmm." Cass sighed. That mouth of his was absolute trouble. "We didn't officially meet, did we. I'm Cassandra Dorsey. Some people call me Cass."

"Cassandra, it's my pleasure."

Her name on his lips, said in his steady deep voice — she might melt back into a puddle. Except her stomach ached. She was famished. "I'm ready to get out of this embarrassing situation. And I would like your help." Cass reached out to him.

He didn't wait for her to change her mind. Instead, he put one of his strong hands in hers and the other under her shoulder. Bullet stood too, then flopped his front body down low on his paws with his butt sticking up in the air and gave out a playful bark.

"He's the funniest thing."

"He thinks it's playtime. All the time. Lead the way, Bullet. Go!" Adam commanded and Bullet shot out of the bathroom and slid down the hall into the wall before he rolled over and tried to scramble to his feet.

"Oh!" She laughed at his klutziness. "What kind of dog is he?" she asked. Adam carefully led her into the living room.

"Part Lab and part hound, not completely sure about the rest. Someone left him on the side of the road, tied to a tree. He was crying like a baby. As soon as I got him free, he shot like a bullet into my truck, claiming me. The only thing I'm certain about is that he's one hundred percent goofball."

"Good God!"

"Are you okay?" Adam clenched his arm around her waist to steady her. His body was so warm against hers that she wanted to lean closer until all of her was attached to him, surrounded by his heat, but some amazing aroma kept her from plastering herself to him like an idiot.

"I'm fine, I think. What smells so damn good?"

He didn't loosen his hold on her until she was at the couch. Gently he nudged her down onto the oversized plush cushions. "Chicken soft tacos. Probably still warm. I'll fix you a plate."

"Yes, please." Bullet jumped up right next to her on the couch and rolled onto his back again, begging for more caresses.

"I should have named you Shameless, you mutt." Adam rubbed the dog's belly. "Stay and keep our lady comfortable while I get dinner." Then he leaned closer to his dog and pretended to whisper, "Try to behave better than you did this morning. We want her to like us."

I like you, Cass almost said as his hair kissed her neck and she breathed in his fresh soapy scent. *Like* felt easy as if they were in elementary school, passing silly notes back and forth. Maybe that was what she should work on, things that were comfortable and silly. Emotions she could ease her way into. Anything was better than grief or the reckless path she'd been on for the past few months. And anything more serious than *like* honestly freaked her out.

Chapter Seven

"I brought beer, but I'm guessing that's not up your alley right now," Adam called from the kitchen. The cottage had an open floor plan, but her back was to him. Christ, he needed a minute. *Now I'm lightheaded. Something about her presence zaps my insides into high speed. 'Something' is too mundane a word. Everything.* His heart needed a jump start after he'd found her unconscious on the floor.

"I'll pass on the beer. I'm freezing," she said as she wrapped the throw blanket around her shoulders.

Pull yourself together. Adam fumbled the tea bags on the counter. *It's food and conversation. Nothing could be worse than your first encounter.* That eased his racing pulse. A bit.

Cassandra, tucked into the oversized couch with a soft knitted afghan wrapped around her shoulders, his puppy sprawled across her legs and her eyes closed with a peaceful look on her face — the first one he'd seen since he met her — settled him. Sparks still hummed through his blood, but Adam's nerves and worry eased. He tried to memorize the serene moment.

"Here you go." Handing her a cup of tea, he pulled Bullet away. "I'll put him on his leash outside while we eat. If that's okay? He might cry like a baby, but better than him scavenging your tacos."

Cass pulled the mug to her nose she inhaled the fragrant tea. "Wow," she whispered.

You said it.

"This tea is like nirvana."

"Do you faint often, like that?"

She paused to take a sip of tea, her expression thoughtful. "Not ever, really. It's weird. I've been exhausted and woozy the last few days. It's like my body knows I came here to rest and found it safe to collapse. You know, like it realized it didn't have to bear the weight of burdens anymore?"

He came back with a tray, handed her a plate and sat next to her, but with a bit of space between them. If she could hear the galloping of his heart, she took pity on him and didn't comment. Adam didn't consider himself a buffoon, but this morning, he'd aced that identity. It was foreign. He felt compelled to be near her and simultaneously as though he had no clue how to behave.

"You have a lot of burdens?" Were those the stories she tried to hide deep in her brown eyes?

"A few, I guess. I...don't know if burdens is the right word. I...I tried to bury a lot of junk. But it turns out I can't ignore serious issues and imagine they'll go away on their own. I actually have to deal with them. Shocking, right?" Her mouth tipped up on the right for a second, a weak smile that didn't reach her tired eyes, exposing loneliness and sadness and confusion to him, before she composed herself again. Like she was shaking off ghosts.

They ate in silence for a few moments. Adam snuck a few glances, but she was one hundred percent concentrating on her food. "This is one of *the best* things I've ever tasted. The chilis and lime, and those grilled onions. My goodness! Perfectly sweet and savory at the same time."

Everything out of her mouth was a seduction. Lips meant for some serious kissing. He nearly choked on his taco. Maybe if he kept *his* mouth full, he wouldn't lose his cool. Her beauty made him delirious.

"Are these homemade tortilla chips?" She licked the salt off her fingers and made a smacking sound.

"Huh?" His brain clicked into buffoon mode. "Uh, yeah. My friends own a Mexican restaurant in Graciella. They taught my sister-in-law how to make them."

"It's amazing to be stuffed from such a delicious meal."

"I'm not sure if anyone would believe me if I told them," Adam said, "but you ate twice as much as I did."

"It was incredible." She met his eyes. "Thank you."

"My pleasure." Taking her plate, he said, "Good food is a big deal for us. If you're here for a while and you want company and more meals like that, you don't have far to go to find them. My mom and Miranda will be thrilled. Miranda is my brother's new wife. The only negative is once they hear how you devoured their tacos. They'll be bugging you to try all their dishes and rave about them."

"I'd love to." She spoke as if he'd offered her a private trip to the moon and back, her greatest wish come true. "It's what I do, actually. Or did until...I mean, I write about food. I'll happily be their guinea pig."

"Don't feel like you have to. I realize I have no idea why you came to Brockman Farms and here I am pushing my family and our business on you."

"I actually read about you...your farm in *Travel Oregon*. I'd love to learn more about the café and barn dinners. Besides, I'm pretty much a part of the farm family now that I've been anointed with your organic compost," she teased.

He let out a sigh and smiled. *At least she's joking about it now.* "I am never going to be able to live that down, am I?"

"Mmm, a few more plates of seriously amazing food and I'll promise to forget it ever happened."

I won't. Adam grasped for her hips beneath his hands as if he held her again. *I won't ever forget.*

"Are you okay?" She studied him.

Adam blinked himself back to the living room in Kilrush. "Yep. Sorry. I'm distracted tonight."

"Right...I...you probably still have stuff to do." She rested her head on the side pillow and dragged her feet up to stretch the length of the couch, snuggling herself under the blanket.

Stuff? He wanted to kiss her right now, with that lazy pleased look on her face. Soft in the lamplight. Instead, Adam bolted into the kitchen. He had to get out of here. "Okay. I'm going to clean up and get Bullet. We'll come in and say goodbye before we head home."

She was nearly asleep when Bullet climbed onto the couch and settled himself next to her.

"Want me to carry you to your bed?" he whispered.

Cass shook her head. "I'm so good here."

A peace surrounded her. Maybe someday she'd let him carry her to bed. Adam shook his head. *Mind out of the gutter, dude. What is wrong with you?*

"Come on, pal. Time to get out of her hair." He tried to pull Bullet off, but Cass' arm wrapped around his dog and Bullet snuggled in to stay.

"I can't decide if this makes you a traitor or a really good dog, buddy." Adam debated dragging his pup with him, but what harm could it do? Maybe she wanted the comfort, and Bullet would let her know if he needed out. "I left my phone number in case you faint again or if you need anything. I'll see you later," he whispered. He got no reply except the sound of her sleeping.

A sky full of brilliant stars lit his way back to his Airstream in the old pasture at the uppermost part of Brockman Farms. Here he was, a simple man who knew the land, who knew animals. That was his life. Smoke from the firepit at the big house scented the chilly night air and voices carried from his family still enjoying their evening together. If he wanted, he could join them again, find warmth and laughter around the fire until they all wandered home. But he sought to be alone instead. Solitude had been his best friend since his brothers left Graciella all those years ago. He'd grown to depend on it for his best thinking and problem-solving.

Adam Brockman might be partial owner in a successful organic farm and new business, something he was extremely proud of, but tonight under the vast tapestry, he felt how small he really was, and every one of his limitations. A man who was more at ease with horses than people. Although it was by choice until the land held his name, he still lived in his trailer. And he could barely carry on a coherent conversation with the prettiest woman he'd ever met. Jesus, he couldn't even cook for her. What could he offer Cassandra Dorsey with her career in a big fancy city hours away from here?

He knew what he wanted to offer. And now he had to figure out if he could make it enough, a life truly worthy of her. What Adam Brockman didn't find strange or difficult to understand was that he knew from the first few minutes of being with her that he wanted to belong to her.

Chapter Eight

For the first time in the canyons of emptiness she'd lived through, Cass woke warm and cozy. She let out a relaxed sigh and savored that deliciousness for a moment before she opened her eyes and found Bullet tucked in tight to her side, his velvety soft ear lightly flicking against her skin. Nestled under her arm, he was stretched out on his back with his hind legs splayed open, completely ridiculous and cute the way only a puppy could be in that position.

"You are a goofball, aren't you?"

His body jerked and with no grace whatsoever, he twitched and fell off the couch, bouncing right back up and putting his paws on the cushion by her face, his tongue hanging out as if to say, "I meant to do that." Then he licked her face and darted to the front door, wagging his entire body and whining.

She'd actually made a dent in catching up on her sleep debt. The sun shone in through all the windows, lighting up the room. In addition to the afghan, she'd been tucked in with an extra blanket. There was a note on the coffee table, held in place with a small jar of late-season dahlias so dark purple they were almost black.

Bullet wouldn't leave your side last night. In the morning you can let him out your front door and he'll find me down at the barns. I'm his meal ticket and aside from chasing the seagulls on the beach, food is his main hobby. If you need anything before that, call. Thanks for sharing dinner with me last night. Adam.

He'd written his phone number next to it.

Holy hell! She'd slept through the night with Adam's dog. But before that, she'd eaten a meal with him, a complete stranger. No, a nice, beautiful man. And he'd thanked her as if she'd done *him* a favor. Most people hadn't been able to be around her the last few months. She understood. She didn't much like being around herself. Last night he'd said he wanted to share not only his meal but his family. Why? Was he attracted to her? Could it be her first two fabulous impressions she'd made on him? One being a first-class snob and the other passed out cold and clammy on the bathroom floor with a wet rag stuck to her head? She could write a book on how attractive all that was.

Even though he'd just met her, he'd left his precious dog with her overnight. He'd taken care of her. Man and dog both had. Cass wasn't sure whether she should be freaked out right now or not. Sharing a cozy meal with a cute man and keeping his dog tucked in tight to her side did not at all go with her plan to heal herself, to get her life on track.

Although, taking into consideration the last few months, she'd done a piss-poor job of caring for herself.

But making commitments, creating space for new people in her life right now, did she want that? *I don't have enough strength to solve that puzzle right now.*

What settled into her was the knowledge that she didn't want to leave this place, not yet. From the minute she'd stepped out of her car, it had wrapped around her like a warm hug. She was starting to sleep well. The water and land had restored her senses. Most importantly, she breathed a measure of letting go, *finally*, and with that, hopefully a path leading back to herself.

Cass rubbed her eyes. *Too much thinking.*

Bullet barked again from the door. All right, she'd make herself chill for now and do what always got her through, taking things step by step. She'd barely opened the front door when Bullet, true to his namesake, shot off the porch, ignoring the steps completely and was out of sight before she could take a breath. She'd intended to grab his leash and walk him down to the barns to make sure he got there safely. *"He'll find me."* Adam's words drifted back into her mind. Hopefully the golden nugget wouldn't splatter anyone with manure today. That brought a smile to her face.

I want someone to find me. Cass stood there, warming in the late morning sun that lazed across the steps and the porch. She'd been surviving in such a cold vacuum, so now to have the rays reach into her body and soul, Cass cherished every moment to let the warmth surround her.

Inside the cottage, built-in shelves lined both sides of the fireplace. Cass ran her hands over the worn spines. A delicious-sounding mystery series by Deanna Raybourn and a poetry collection of Lucille Clifton's graced the shelves, along with books by some authors she wasn't familiar with.

Pat Benatar's *We Belong* blared from her phone and Cass grinned. "Nicely done, Annabelle." She and her sister-in-law had started changing each other's ring tones back in college in an attempt to out-embarrass each other. Now they did it with fun songs that wouldn't get either of them fired or kicked out of a journalism lecture like *Me So Horny* had done to Cass senior year.

"It's kinda tame, though." Cass could hear Annie typing away at her computer. "I could dig up some doozies now that you're jobless."

"Ahh, I can feel the love."

Annie giggled. "You were supposed to call me and tell me you arrived somewhere safely, missy."

"I te—"

"And don't give me that impersonal text crap. I was worried you'd drive straight into the ocean."

"Annie," Cass sighed. "I'm not in that darkest of places anymore. You don't have to worry so much."

"I will always worry about you, dammit. And I know you needed to get away. I'm proud of you. I just…I miss you."

Cass had to force the tears back. "I've only been gone three days."

"You know what I mean. Don't be a dummy." Two PhDs in finance and mathematics and her best friend still threw insults like a four-year-old. It softened the edge of Cass' guilt.

"I promise I'm climbing out of the numbness. I'm in a beautiful place. I'm going to recharge and take my life back."

"Oh yeah, where are you and what are you doing? Give me all the details before my next class.

"I think I'm going to sit outside on the gorgeous front porch of a charming cottage at Brockman Farms in the sunshine and lose myself in a book." The one that had caught her interest but which she'd been too tired to dive into yet was *Coming Home* by Rosamond Pilcher, a sweeping epic about a girl growing up during a time of war, facing love and sadness and finally finding a place to call home. Cass was trying to make her way back home, to remember what it felt like.

The pleasure of reading peacefully was another sacrifice of her grief. She'd quit being able to relax enough to enjoy a story. All these things she'd let sorrow and irritability take from her. Recapturing the joy of good books was a baby step she'd relish taking today.

"Thrilling. Really. I liked my idea better, pools, cocktails and hot men."

There is one particularly hot man here.

"Oh, time to go crush my students' egos with an exam. Listen, sister, you pick up that phone and call me. C-A-L-L. No texting bullshit. I need to hear your voice."

"'Kay, Annie, love you."

"Love you too, Cassie." Annabelle made kissing noises before she hung up.

Even though she lived in the apartment directly below Annabelle and Cass' brother Garrett, she might as well have been on Mars for how much of a zombie she'd been. One more aspect of her life to renovate, her relationships with the people who had held her hand through everything.

Maybe whatever stress her body was purging was finally coming to an end. Last night she'd devoured two huge servings of tacos, and she was hungry again. All good signs she was healing, growing stronger and could beat the toll stress insisted on taking on her. Intense sea-blue eyes brought another smile to her face. She really should make sure Bullet found his human again. If it meant Cass got to see his human again too, she wouldn't complain. But before she did anything else, she needed a seriously long hot shower.

Cass stripped and let the powerful spray perform its own kind of magic. She closed her eyes and luxuriated with another lush soap. This time jasmine burst forth around her, seductive dreamy scent. *This shower's big enough for two and I know exactly who I'd like to share it with.*

Whoa. She braced her hand against the wall and let the water sluice over her back. Where had that thought come from? Showers had a way of cleansing her mind and it was easy to let down her guard. Except now she wasn't weeping in sorrow, but fantasizing about Adam Brockman joining her under the delicious water. Desire raced through her. Her nipples tightened and ached and her core throbbed with need.

Cass hummed in anticipation. What harm could it do? Closing her eyes, she let her fantasy flow. She imagined a strong naked farmer stepping in with her to wash her back while his hands slipped around to her front and pulled her tight against his wet body. His heat seared through the steamy, seductive water connecting them, making her skin and blood hum and ache. *Cass* ached. She ran the soap over her body, hot and flush from so much more than water and steam.

Alive and needy, she dropped the sponge and used her fingers to roam her slippery, soapy skin, imagining Adam's large hands. Would he be a gentle giant or a frenzy of desire like what burned from her right this moment? Maybe he'd dig those hands into her hips and bring her even closer so their soapy bodies collided. Hard and soft, hot and wet. She moved her fingers over her breasts and belly, each touch setting off a new sharp firework. Cass dipped lower as she imagined him sinking into her, his own head thrown back in ecstasy. And when she connected with her wet, soft folds, she exploded in a rush of sensation and longing and breath. *Holy wow! That came out of nowhere.* Cass leaned her cheek against the shower wall and smiled as she came down from her high.

Phew! I guess when my senses return, they barrel right back in at full speed. Scent, hunger, exhaustion, warmth, joy, lust. How wonderful to feel again. A shiver caught her off guard. *How scary too.*

Cass turned the water off and grabbed a towel. The way her mind conjured Adam, naked, stoked her body, like a live wire, to an exploding orgasm. The way her heart tried to beat through her ribs. The beauty and staid foundation of this place and what it meant to those who lived here. *Getting my life back together.* None of those were things to treat casually. Cass needed to tread very, very carefully with the wonderful people of Brockman Farms. And, most importantly, if the last few months had taught her anything it was that she needed to tread carefully with her own battered heart.

Chapter Nine

"Whoa, buddy!" Cruz Brockman yelled as Bullet shot down the hill. "Adam. Your dog finally arrived. Where's he been all morning?"

"He spent the night at Cass'." Adam reached down and scrubbed his dog's fur. "Hey, bud, how's our new friend? Bet you want some breakfast." At that word, Bullet wiggled his entire body and danced around Adam, barking his demands. Adam led Bullet into the barn where he had a food bowl for him and caught the shock on Cruz's face. He grinned and kept on walking.

"Oh, no you don't." Cruz followed him.

"You have questions. Ask away." Adam grabbed Bullet's bowl and filled it with food then grabbed the rubber buckets to fill with his special mix of rice bran and pulp for the malnourished horses he'd rescued from an old farm in Medford. The owners had died and the horses had been abandoned. It made him sick to think of it.

"Cass? The guest at Kilrush. The one you attacked with manure. The one you took dinner to. You spent the night." His tone was sharp, and Adam didn't like the implication at all, even or especially coming from his brother. "You can't sleep with the guests."

"Those aren't questions, Cruz." Adam gripped the bin and curbed his temper before the horses sensed his mood. His voice lost the teasing. "All I did was take her dinner and check on her. Bullet's the only one who spent the night."

"Sorry, I… That was uncalled for."

"Apology accepted." Adam barreled through life completely open and honest, working hard every day. He might have been fun-loving and full of laughter, but he was also driven and stubborn and he knew what he wanted. He absolutely would not take advantage of any woman, especially one alone and exhausted. "But I'd like to have dinner with her again, and again. And more than that." It might have been too simple for others to understand, but to him it felt like fate.

"You don't know anything about her. And she's a *guest*, Adam." Cruz's words held a warning again.

"I heard you," he fired back, his voice quiet but clipped. Adam could be just as severe. "I'm not going to take advantage of anyone. I'm also not stupid and I know my heart and mind. When have I ever *not* known what I wanted in life? And when have I ever been wishy-washy about getting what I want?" He let out a frustrated sigh. Maybe his brothers didn't know. They'd been gone a long time.

"This isn't taking care of a farm or raising horses or building your own house. This is a person we're talking about, a person you met yesterday."

"Stop. I respect you, brother, but please don't insult me. She's going through something serious. I found her collapsed on the bathroom floor when I got there last night. She was so exhausted that she didn't have enough energy to get herself up and fed. Bullet wouldn't leave her side. She loved the tacos. Seemed surprised to enjoy food. Ate more than I did. I feel both excited and extremely stupid in her presence. Something stuttered to life in me, and I'd like to get to know her more, if she wants that." *Damn, I hope she wants that.* "But I'm not going to maul her or force her into anything.

"Couldn't get Bullet to leave so I left him there to watch over her. All I care about now is whether or not she's okay. I'll find out the rest when she's ready to share. You're right. Knowing the work I want to do, or the design of the house I want to build are easier things to aim for and achieve, but I also want to build a life with someone I love, like you. Our father was a bastard, Cruz, but I didn't let his behavior jade my beliefs in love, not like you and Turner. I've always longed for it, and I've always sensed I would recognize my person when she appeared. So please don't get all older-brother's-here-to-tell-you-how-to-be-a-man."

Cruz rubbed his hand over his face. "Apparently being the all-knowing, lecturing older brother comes back easily to me."

Adam slung his arm around Cruz and smiled as they walked back into the sunlight. Cruz might have been the oldest, but at over six-and-a-half-feet and two-hundred fifty pounds, Adam was still the biggest of the Brockman brothers. "Since when have you been all-knowing?"

"Ha." Cruz laughed and elbowed him hard in the ribs. "Excited and stupid, huh? After only meeting her yesterday?" Cruz's smile grew huge. "You are in for a ride, brother."

Adam pretended to cough at the hit to his ribs and tackled Cruz into the dirt.

"Christ, I forget you're the size of a tractor." Cruz barely got the words out as they wrestled, and Adam had him pinned again, nearly taking his breath away.

"Do you boys actually enjoy that?"

"Ah, love, come give me a kiss, will you?" Cruz beckoned his wife, Miranda, as she walked toward the barn.

"Not on your life. You'll pull me right down with you," Miranda said.

"Come on, you'll be just as pretty down here with me."

"Not covered in dirt and hay."

"Wanna find out?" Cruz reached up to grab her, but she stepped out of reach, her laughter filling the air around them.

If this was the ride Cruz meant, Adam wanted every second of it. "Wait, do I smell muffins? She brought us muffins. Leave her alone." Adam shoved Cruz away.

"Always thinking with your stomach." Cruz cuffed him on the side of the head.

"Not always," Adam said. He looked past Cruz. "Mornin', Cassandra." Her gaze stroked his skin like the warming sun after a long, bitter winter. He smiled. *She looks better. The dark circles are gone.* She stared at them as if they'd each grown a tail and horns.

She gave a small wave. "I thought you might need Bullet's leash. He took off without it this morning. Are you all right?"

"No, they're not. Hi, I'm Miranda. They're bonkers. They think wrestling in the dirt to prove their manhood is a sport."

"It isn't?" Cruz asked, getting up and stalking Miranda.

"You're..." She could barely talk through her laughter and squeals. "You're filthy, your hair's a mess and Adam pinned you again which means you'll probably have bruises."

"I let him win so you'll take care of me." He grabbed her in a hug and gave her a loud smacking kiss on the lips. "Gonna take care of me?"

"Cruz." She laughed as he walked her toward the barn. "Stop, you'll squish the muffins and I think you're making our guest nervous."

He kept his arm around Miranda, but he stopped walking her backward and smiled at Cass. "Sorry, I got distracted. I'm Cruz. Don't think we've met yet."

"What smells so damn delicious?" Cass quickly covered her mouth. "Wow, overdramatic much?"

"It's okay," Adam broke in. He sprang to his feet. "Miranda's muffins are drool-worthy. They make us all act loony. What kind are they this morning?"

"They're pumpkin, with lots of clove and nutmeg and a hint of maple syrup. I'm trying out some new fall and winter recipes. There's plenty here, Cass, would you like one?"

"The scent is driving me crazy. I don't think I can say no."

Miranda opened the basket. Cruz and Adam started to reach in too, but she shooed them. "No way. Go wash your hands. I want you to enjoy my muffins, not dry, caked-on dirt and hay and horse food and whatever else is all over you."

Cass watched the men walk away. "Do they always act like that?" She couldn't hide the surprise in her voice.

"They do now. I get the feeling they were like that at times when they were kids. I'm still learning more about them every day myself. I've only been here since April. Cruz was moody then with a hard shell around him. Their father was not a nice man, and from what I've heard, that's putting it mildly."

"They're oddly okay with fighting?"

"To them it's playing, teasing. They love each other to pieces." Miranda smiled at Cass.

"And you," Cass said quietly. "I get the impression they love you to pieces too." As soon as the words left her mouth, Miranda's expression lit up. The woman glowed with happiness. It wrapped around her, the aura of this place.

Cass bit her muffin to stop any embarrassing words from exiting her mouth about glowing auras. "Seriously! This muffin! This is like heaven."

"I like you already, Cass," Miranda said through her laughter.

"I mean it. This is… Can I have another one? My appetite has been so nonexistent that I forgot what delicious muffins, delicious *anything* tasted like. It's actually been a long time since I enjoyed food at all. But last night with the tacos Adam brought and now these. I… There goes my mouth again." Cass covered her eyes. Heat crept up her neck. It was like her mouth had a mind of its own spilling out whatever entered her head. Where had her careful filter gone, her protective quiet?

"It's this place and the people. I swear, you'll probably think I'm crazy but it's magical. It hit me too when I came, like all my senses were busted open," Miranda said.

"But I came here to get my focus back, to regroup, I think." Cass searched Miranda's eyes. "Well, I'm not really sure."

"I know what you mean." Miranda's voice was serious but kind, like she was talking to a good friend. "I mean I don't know what you've been through, but I came here intent on completing an audit. I was completely closed off, lonely and suffering, although I didn't realize all of that. And this place…" Miranda swept her hand around. "It squeezed my heart and made me want to be alive. Sometimes the journey takes us and not the other way around."

Want to be alive. Exactly. Cass wanted so hard to be alive. At the least, she sure could use a step up from drowning in grief, or the more recent rash and stupid.

"You probably think I'm crazy." Miranda, clearly not offended, smiled at Cass.

Cass shook her head. What could she say? She hardly knew this woman. *Can we be friends?* That might make *her* the one with a few screws loose. "You look happy. I don't know what that's like anymore."

"Stay long enough and this place will show you," Miranda invited. The men were coming back out of the barn. "I have to get to the kitchen. I'm practicing making pastry dough. Cass, you're welcome to join me?"

"You're stealing her away?" Adam asked, pointing his gaze in her direction. "Don't you want to meet my girl?" He grabbed a muffin out of Miranda's basket.

Miranda wanted her company, and so did Adam? Maybe this place was enchanted.

"You have a girl?"

"Come walk with me and I'll show you. You saw her last night. Gracie." Dusty work clothes, a baseball hat on his head, his face sun warmed and sweaty, and still she had to remind herself to breathe at his beauty. His eyes were like the bluest ocean she could drift away on. Memories of her shower brought a flush up her neck. *Nope, can't go there right now. Food writing, that's my mantra. My body might want him, but my brain needs inspiration.* Being invited to cook in the Brockman House kitchen was an opportunity she'd be a fool to pass up. And at least when it came to her career, Cass was no fool.

"You can bake with me anytime you want, Cass." Miranda interrupted her thoughts. She stood in front of Cruz, who had his arms around her and was sneaking another muffin. "We're using the pastry to make croissants."

"The last time I had a croissant was on my sixteenth birthday when my mother took me to Paris. It was February, bitter cold and rainy, and we warmed up in this tiny bakery with the best coffee of my life and a basket of croissants. It was dreamy. So good, so flakey and buttery."

"I'm not sure we can compete with that lovely memory, but maybe we can make a new one. It'll be my first time making them and I'd love the company."

Although she'd read about their ideals to create a warm community-like atmosphere at Brockman Farms, Cass hadn't expected to be so welcomed. Perhaps Miranda was right. The journey would take her.

"Ha! She's picking croissants over horses." Cruz elbowed Adam. Adam smiled with a confidence that nearly had her swaying and swooning. *Holy wow, his aura is powerful.*

"I think I'd like to join you, Miranda," she said while the eye contact between Adam and her sizzled and sparked. *Best catch my breath before I dive off the cliff headfirst.*

Chapter Ten

Cassandra couldn't remember the last time she'd had so much fun in a kitchen. She was an accomplished chef in her own right, a food snob for sure with — once upon a time — a sharp sense of what brought a meal to exquisite perfection. She'd been tasting and writing about food for over a decade.

But she'd been so focused on climbing the ladder of food writing in San Francisco — not that she ever would have gotten where she had without that focus and determination, especially as a woman. But today she'd laughed, sat in cozy chairs by a fireplace in a kitchen with tea and gossip and got her hands messy making dough.

It reminded her of baking with her mom and grandmother. A simple, fulfilling task, with so few ingredients, it only occurred to her now on her walk back to her cottage. No specialty spices only sold at the top of a mountain in Patagonia. No five-star soup with twenty-seven ingredients. No foam of scallops made into a snowman. Simply flour, butter, water. Lots and lots of butter. *Mmm* and such good butter, from their own cream here on the farm.

Her brain was on fire with ideas for articles, the homegrown idea, could pastry have a terroir, family business, all different members, new and old. The comfort of it all. Her fingertips vibrated with the need to type. A glass of wine, the cozy oversized chair and her laptop had her name written all over them. She could write for hours. And the best part was that the scent of baked pastry clung to her sweater. Well aside from the croissants they'd sent home with her. Could a person live on croissants alone? Cass unlocked her cottage door and was stepping inside when a half bark, half whimper startled her.

"Oh, my goodness." She set the bag of goodies down and held her hands toward Bullet. "Good boy, Bullet. Stay." She used her softest voice and tried to make the dog believe her words so he'd stay sitting and not spring himself on her as he loved to do. She didn't have an entire wardrobe to toss at his expense. Instead of jumping, he hobbled over to her whimpering. Covered in sea water and sand and dirt and...

"Bullet, are you bleeding?" Ignoring the cost to her clothes, Cass knelt immediately and cuddled him. Lifting one of his paws, she exposed a dirty, bloody wound.

The lazy summers she'd helped her grandparents with their farm animals rushed back in and she hurried into caretaking mode. Nudging Bullet into her lap, she carefully rose with his heavy, shivering body and carried him into the bathroom, kicking the door shut in case he tried to escape.

"Okay, sugar, we're going to give you a bath." Bullet clung to her as she turned on the warm water. When she set him in, she took it as a good sign that he didn't bolt or freak out, but she worked quickly to rinse him off because he wasn't exactly happy either. The poor dog had frozen in place. "I know you don't like this slippery surface. We're almost done. How long have you been hiding under my bush waiting for me, silly boy? You're freezing."

Cass grabbed a bunch of towels and wrapped him up to dry his soaking body, but he leaped out of the tub like a lunatic, spraying water everywhere, and yelped when he put pressure on his paw.

"It's a good thing you're super cute and I'm already half in love with you, because that's another outfit you owe me. Now sit."

Bullet shot his butt to the floor and allowed Cass to inspect his leg. "Looks like you have a piece of glass stuck in there. And I don't know what you'll do if I try and get it out. Let's call your dad, huh?"

He let her pick him up and carry him to the couch and by the time Adam walked in, all six feet several inches of gorgeous, worry covering his handsome face, Bullet was crashed out asleep on her lap.

"Well," Adam said, pausing in the doorway. "I'm not sure why you're still here after the stellar welcome we've given you, but thank you. Mind if I sit?"

Always with the sexy courtesy. She could get used to a farmer's manners.

"Please. I'm surprised this lump isn't jumping at the sound of your voice."

"Sleeping is one of his favorite activities. He's a champion. Where did you find him?" Adam ran his hand through the crazy fur on Bullet's neck, right where Cass' hand rested.

"He was hovering under the bushes when I got home. His right paw is hurt. Poor thing was covered in wet sand."

"Poor thing, my butt. He chases the seagulls down at the beach like a mad man and gets surprised every single time a wave crashes him. Got a bit of glass in there, don't cha, boy?" The man might have acted annoyed at his dog's antics, but love flowed through his gentle touch, the crooning, soft words. He'd raced back here from a meeting in town. This was true love between a man and his mutt.

"Let's get you to the vet." Adam leaned into her and started to put his hands under the dog. "Do you mind if I take him off your lap?" This was the second time they'd found themselves in this awkward position. So awkward that she wanted to lean up and savor those beautiful lips of his. *At least this time I'm not sprawled on the bathroom floor. And at least I'm admitting it now, not that I'm going to do a thing about it. Or am I?*

"No," she said.

"No, you don't mind, or you do? You're angry all the sudden."

He wasn't angry or confused or flushed. There he went diving into her eyes again, searching. "If it's any consolation, I want to kiss you as much as you want to kiss me." His gaze strayed to her lips and he devoured them without one single bite.

"You just put it right out there, don't you? All happy and convinced about it," she said and watched his face light up at her pout.

"I have a great imagination. Plus, you didn't deny you wanted to kiss me. I'm hopeful."

"I'm not sure I have anything to give another person right now, Adam." Her words were a whispered question more than anything else. They said the truth hurts and it sure felt horrible scraping up her throat. Especially when he blinked, put his hands carefully under his dog and took him from her lap. All the warmth left her.

"Well, buddy, time to go."

"Do you want some help?"

"We're good." She couldn't tell if it was dismissal or courtesy. Either way she hated it.

Cass stood and followed them to the door. "I'm sorry, Adam... I... My mind is kind of a muddled mess. You could still be mad at me and let me hold him while you drive. In case he wakes up."

At least his smile didn't appear forced. "No worries, Cass. I'm not mad. Javier's our unofficial vet. He's meeting me down at the barns. Short walk. No car ride needed." He *said* he wasn't mad, so why was she all tangled up inside? She owed him nothing, but something in his gaze sang of a tightly leashed longing and caressed her skin with the message he belonged to her. Or wanted to. *Silly notions. No one belongs to you.*

"Do you want help anyway?" It didn't sit right with her, parting like this. Why had she blurted out her situation? Because something about him pulled out the honesty in her. Plus, she might not have much to offer someone, but she was damn tired of being alone.

"I'd always enjoy your company, and it's a pretty night for a walk." The curse of a young, naive man with the entire world stretched out in front of him. He believed wholeheartedly in the positive. Had she ever held a belief so strong?

"You might need your jacket. Wind kicked up."

Grabbing her sweatshirt, she locked up and followed Adam. The light was fading but along the path where he'd been planting and laying compost were little low lights. Smart, efficient, great for anyone wandering at night. "You've all done a wonderful job with your farm and the renovations. It's beautiful here, like a painting."

"Glad you like it. Different than a big city. How do you do it? Live so close to so many people and cars and roads and buildings." Adam's shudder made her grin. She might as well have snuck a spider down his neck.

"San Francisco is amazing. The culture, the location, so many different kinds of people, the art and food," she sighed. Cass hadn't really enjoyed her city in a while now. *I miss it. I think.* "Have you ever been?"

"Nope. Cruz and Turner are the travelers. I can count on one hand the states I've visited."

"One hand?" Cass had been all over the world. "Sorry I didn't mean to sound so shocked. Okay, yes I did. You don't like to travel?"

"It's more about not wanting to leave here. Everything I love is on the farm, in Graciella, the coast. Can't imagine anyplace more beautiful than this."

Snorkeling in the ice blue waters of the Great Barrier Reef, the towering bamboo forests in China, Gaudi's art shimmering across the city of Barcelona. It was charming here, certainly, but to never explore the rest of the world? A grumble startled her.

"Is that Bullet?"

Adam's deep chuckle sang through the night. "Snores like a drunken man."

She laughed with him. The temperature had dipped with the chilly wind and Cass stayed close to Adam's side. His warmth was a lure she molded toward in the darkness.

"Something about baths. He hates them. Acts like a wounded soldier afterward. He's gained more weight too. Growing pains and trauma will take it out of a mutt."

"You were right — it is a nice night for a walk." She liked listening to him. His voice anchored her, as though even with her eyes closed she could find him if he called to her. The chill had moved in and opened up a new bouquet. "It smells like the end of fall finally, cold and dry," she whispered, entranced again by the way scents exploded around her as they walked through the apple trees.

"It's like we turned a corner, isn't it?"

Seasonally? Or in our newly weird 'I just met you but you smell really, really good and I'm super attracted to you' relationship? "Mmm-hmm."

"You know, Cassandra," Adam began as they reached one of the large barns. A song. Her name was a song on his lips. "Sometimes it's better to ask what your heart wants."

"Pardon?" His words stopped her. And he continued effortlessly, casually as if he hadn't blasted her with a heavy-duty question.

"You said your mind was a mess. What about your heart?"

My heart is still buried under debris. Although maybe it had begun to climb back out.

Chapter Eleven

"What did the pup do to himself?" Javier opened the office door and led them back into his clinic room.

"He tangled with some broken glass. Javier, this is Cassandra. She gave him a bath but left the paw for us."

"Smart woman. Can't predict how an animal in pain will react. Adam, get a good hold on him while I see if it's easy enough to pull out with tweezers."

Smart, sexy, beautiful, stubborn, prickly, wounded. What else? He wanted to know every side of her. It might have been forward, asking her what beat in her heart, especially after her confession, but how else should a person go through life? The heart was as important as the mind. More so for Adam.

"I'm still hoping he'll like me when this is over." Cass gestured toward Bullet. Why did he think she was talking to him? *I'm half in love with you already. We passed* like *when you yelled at me over compost.* In her presence he felt twisted up like fun mirrors at a circus.

He'd best concentrate on his mutt right now. "Hey, buddy," he said. "No telling what you'll do if you wake up in the middle of this." Bullet started and tried to get out of his arms, but eventually settled for slathering his tongue all over Adam's hand.

"Ms. Cassandra, can you grab a big soup bone from that basket?" Javier asked her. "If you could fill it with the peanut butter, next to it, we'll give that to our patient to hopefully distract him."

"Absolutely. Please call me Cass."

She hadn't asked Adam to call her Cass. He liked her full name. It fit her, expansive, full of brilliance.

Overall, Bullet behaved much better than Adam had anticipated. Better even than Adam, who was happy to have a fifty-pound mutt to hold down to channel his concern. It didn't matter how crazy Bullet drove him. The soft goofball had burrowed under Adam's skin right to his heart. Taking care of animals and people was in his nature. Bullet's soul was funny and good and loving. It hadn't been a choice really, since that first day months ago when he'd leapt into Adam's truck and fallen asleep on the passenger seat before Adam had even started driving.

Poor guy—Cass had been right—was crashed out from the experience and the painkiller Javier had given him from having to clean the wound and stitch it. The cut wasn't deep, thank goodness, but lord knew how long Bullet had played in the sand and mud with it slashed open. He'd need a good night's rest in the crate in Javier's office with his paw bandaged. And the cone of shame around his neck. At least Javier had a new kind of cone that was more like a big soft donut. Donut would have been a great name for Bullet. *Or Doofus.*

"I'll walk you home." Cass had weathered the whole thing well, Bullet's yelping and whining. The mutt's obvious distress had nearly brought Adam to tears.

"You don't have to. I know the way," she said.

"It's too dark for you to walk alone. I wouldn't feel right."

She nodded, but not before he caught her smile. So she'd indulge him. He didn't want her to indulge him, the swoony, ridiculous farmer...even though that description fit him perfectly. For God's sake, he was so twisted up. No, not true. He knew what he wanted, in which direction his life was pointed. How did he convince her to join him? The question had beat through his blood since he'd first touched her.

"It takes on a different sort of lovely at night. All these layers to your farm," she said.

"Are you falling for it, Cassandra?"

"I think it would be difficult for anyone not to fall for this place, Adam. And now on a clear fall night, with the wind quiet and the stars mimicking the lights you've strewn along the path, and...oh!" She covered her heart with her hand and spun around. "How brilliant. It sparkles. How did you do it?" She strode ahead and inspected the path.

The path to her cottage was much too short for his liking tonight.

"When we poured the concrete, we sprinkled sea glass and fools' gold into the rock mix and"—he paused to laugh—"glitter. Pretty sure the glitter was Lily's idea." The solar lights were necessary. The rest was for beauty. And she reveled in it. His heart clicked into place upon seeing her delight, *his woman's delight,* in a thing so simple. Belonging beat through him again.

Cass grabbed his hand and squeezed. "It was a good one."

"Yes." He squeezed back and gave a gentle tug, urging her toward him. She didn't pull away, but put her hand toward his chest, hesitating a moment before she finally touched him. "You sparkle too."

"Mmm, those are pretty words, Adam."

"I only speak the truth," he said.

"I think anyone would shine here surrounded by glitter. Another little bit of magic."

"You've been listening to Miranda." Adam brought their joined hands up to cover the one on his chest and wrapped his other one around her hip. The crisp air surrounded them, but between them beat a hum of warmth. Her pulse fluttered unsteady under his thumb. Oddly, it steadied his heartbeat.

"Is she wrong?" Cassandra whispered. She was nearly as tall as he was. Sparks flew from her body, and the way their bodies fit was snug and erotic, almost. *If only she'd take one step closer.* And his body came alive. No more circus mirrors turning him upside down. He had one focus, Cassandra Dorsey. Her soft skin, the shimmer in her eyes as they caught the starlight and danced for him. Her intoxicating lips.

Was magical the word? He had been born connected to this land, to this life. Experienced the beauty and hardship and worth in it every day. Took nothing for granted. But this moment, right here under a chandelier of night's beauty, wrapped around Cass, felt like landing on the moon.

"Because I don't know if I believe in magic."

"Supernatural forces aren't your thing?" he teased. "Whatever it is, I feel it too and it strikes me as important enough that I'd regret my whole life if I didn't explore it."

"I *do* want you to kiss me," she admitted, breathless, beautiful, but perhaps uncertain. It held him back. He stroked his finger over hers, wanting to touch her everywhere. But being this close to her made it hard to think. He wanted to take his own advice and listen to his heart, but his heart was being pounded over by his libido, which was acting more like an enamored puppy who wanted to slobber kisses all over her. And listening to that dimwit was not the way he intended to sweet talk Ms. Dorsey. Leaning in, he kissed her forehead, then reluctantly pulled his hands away, giving her arms one soft caress before he stepped back.

He watched as she rubbed her hands up and down her arms. The chill kicked them both now. "I'm not intentionally giving you mixed messages."

"I didn't think you were." Adam shook his head and grinned. "When you're ready, I'd love to take you up on your offer." He had to get away or he'd stalk right over and kiss her until the sun came up. Adam walked backward, memorizing the shape of her silhouetted against her cottage lights.

"Goodnight, Cassandra. Thank you." He put his hand over his heart. "For taking care of my boy." It got him the smile he wanted, wanted to *deserve*, and it chased away the cold and lonely.

"Will you be okay, without him, two nights in a row?"

"I'm heading back to the barns now. I'd be too worried about him to leave him there. Plus if he wakes up whining, he'll drive the horses nuts."

"Give him a kiss for me, will you?"

All he could do was nod. Was she teasing him now? Wicked woman. He could give as good as her.

"Sweet dreams. Think of me." And he turned and headed into the night.

Let her toss and turn all night too.

Chapter Twelve

Exhaustion might as well be her name these days. This morning, however, she knew she could blame it on her terrible night's sleep. She'd spent a long time into the night swooning over Adam, then mentally undressing him. When she'd finally fallen asleep, her dreams had been pure erotic torture. She didn't know whether they'd been a curse, or sweet as Adam had encouraged. *Sweet indeed.* The man wasn't all perfectly nice and smitten and courteous. His deep dark goodnight words had whispered sensual promises to all her body parts that were definitely no longer numb and buried but sorely ignored. *And none too happy about it.*

Her showers, on the other hand, were turning out to be tons of fun. This morning she'd scented her entire body with a musky bergamot and jasmine soap while imagining Adam with her again, his eyes darkening as she'd rubbed the soap all over herself, then rubbed her soapy body all over his. Why in the hell hadn't she kissed him last night? *Really kissed him.* He could be in the shower with her right now.

Too bad she was so wishy-washy in person. *More like scared shitless.* She wasn't only attracted to Adam in a sexual way. He had so many great qualities too. Kindness, patience, humor, belief in all things good and right, loyalty to his beings and his land. Not even Nathan had been so happily set in his world, his foundation. Not many people truly were in today's fast-paced unsettled world. It was attractive. *But is it real?*

She'd planned on reading and relaxing here at Brockman Farms, but had no idea actual food writing inspiration would be flowing. Yesterday in the Brockman kitchen had energized and grounded her. There were few problems a perfect flakey croissant couldn't fix. But there was also so much family fun in the kitchen. Miranda and Katie had formed a warm and obvious bond.

Turner had spent much of the morning working at the large corner banquette. His new office in town was currently being renovated by his wife, Lily, who had also happened to swing by. Cass didn't know if Lily was more interested in the croissants or sneaking a kiss from her fiancé, who could not hide the look of love and luck on his face and who had teased and doted on Lily with equal measure.

Javier and Elena had brought organization and zen to the entire operation even though Javier was only present for a few moments, also to dote on his love, Katie, and steal a pastry.

The pastries were definitely theft-worthy.

And the scents were heavenly. Cass hoped she never lost that gift again.

The family had treated her like she belonged, involving her in the work as much as the conversation. And they hadn't minded a bit when she asked permission to write about them.

And she wanted to write about them. Her only problem this morning was which topic to begin with. She'd take that problem any day.

What had started as an essay about how to make the perfect croissant and how to cut corners for home bakers who might not have as much time had morphed into another essay about Brockman House itself, the history, the new renovations, the soon-to-open café featuring not only amazing meals and goodies, but local artisan wares, wines, pottery. From there ideas of family and warmth and community had drawn Cass into a larger essay. She wanted to know the history of the entire farm, the town of Graciella, its inhabitants. She wanted to know its story.

Love flowed throughout the place. Cass could feel it as sure as her heart beating. Which stuttered to life again. Life and love continued on around her every day. She'd been burrowed under for too long. The magnificent scents bounding back into her environment were proof she didn't want to stay buried. It all led her to another more personal essay about all the nuances lost through grief. Or the way our brains process grief. Perhaps how important the sense of smell is. So many ideas flashed through her mind.

Tea and leftover croissants were her morning companions along with several new drafts of essays. Cass was wrung out and exhilarated at the same time. She wanted to check on Bullet. Both dog and his owner had threaded their way through her mind, even when she'd been caught up in the writing.

Maybe she'd send a text. How awkward could a person be through text?

Cass grabbed her phone and typed.

Cass: Hi, Adam. How is your buddy this morning?

She was warming her tea when her phone chimed.

Adam: Good afternoon, Cassandra. Bullet is fine. Cranky and whiney and he doesn't like the sleeve on his paw, but he'll get over it. How are you on this beautiful day? I've been thinking of you and our walk. I'd like to walk with you at nighttime under the stars again. Sleep well?

Hmph. He was teasing her about her sleep as if he knew. *Maybe his sleep was full of yummy distractions too.* She read his text over and over, imagining the deep sound of his voice and hint of teasing seduction there every time he said her name.

Wait, *good afternoon?* She glanced at the time. After three already. Cass did a little shimmy. *I've been writing for over six hours! About food! Yay, me!*

Cass: I'm good. Thanks for asking. Been writing all morning. Lost track of time. And no. I did not sleep well. I was a little stirred up.

Adam: In a good way? Or a confused way?

She bit her lip and hesitated. They were venturing into careful territory. Did she want to go there with him? Yes, yes she did.

Cass: Both. But I'm not confused anymore. The amazing spa shower helped. The luscious soaps. The multiple spray heads. It's so enormous.

Text teasing was new to her. But before she could second guess or giggle too much, he shot back.

Adam: Ms. Dorsey, you do know there's a fine line between flirting and torture? Now I'm imagining all the places I want to kiss you.

He let her off easy when he continued.

Adam: Hey, I'm needed with one of the horses. Looking forward to seeing you or texting with you later.

Cass flopped back on the couch. *Talk about all stirred up.* The man had her flushing and breathing heavily and he wasn't even in the same room. Well, she couldn't spend all her time in the shower. Although sharing that shower with one sexy man who was not afraid to hide his interest in her was a delicious thought.

How lovely to flirt with him over text. Safe, not out of control. After a dinner of croissant stuffed with maple ham and butter and more cups of the nirvana-like tea they'd gifted the cottage with, Cass wanted a walk. It was nearly impossible not to want to explore more of this gorgeous place, especially in fall, the colors and now the scents exploding around her. If she happened to see Adam, she'd count that as her good luck for the day, especially if he didn't end up showering her with compost. And if he was dirty, she'd be happy to help get him clean in that big-enough-for-two shower upstairs. Now she was hot and bothered all over again.

The day had been warm, but Cass suspected the night would cool again. There were no clouds to insulate them this evening. She wrapped a sweater around herself and stepped onto the porch. Sitting on the woven shamrock welcome mat were the most beautiful cowgirl boots she'd ever seen. *Correction.* The most beautiful boots period. Cass bent down to get a better look. Leather with a dark antique teal finish. Embroidered white curls, flowers and a few stars climbed the boot. Even the insides were adorned with a hint of flourish as the embroidery curled over. Tucked into one was a note rolled up and tied with a green ribbon.

Her hand shook as she opened it and the threat of tears whispered in her eyes again.

Cassandra, these made me think of you, gorgeous, strong, mysterious, enchanting. These are great for wandering around the farm or riding horses, if that interests you. Perhaps these can make up for the ones Bullet and I ruined upon our first meeting. You have to admit, it was quite the first meeting. And because it led me to you, it's a moment I promise never to forget.

They fit perfectly and now that she realized it, her ruined suede ones had disappeared from her porch. So, she could add sneaky to Adam's charms. And those charms were wrapping themselves around her and prodding open her heart. Cass grabbed one of her old socks and tied it in a knot. If Bullet were like most mutts, socks might be one of his favorite toys.

When she reached the barn, it was quieter than she'd assumed. Javier was on the phone but he waved her in. There was one noise she recognized. Tiny but mighty puppy snores came from around the corner. Bullet slept in a crate, belly up, hind legs splayed out. A blue bandaged wrapped around one paw and up his leg. His belly fur was lighter, almost white and curled around the edges in all different directions. *Soft sweet boy.*

"'Evening, Ms. Cassandra," Javier said, his calm voice not even startling the sleeping pup. "Adam and Cruz are still out in the fields, helping with the last of the harvest."

Cass pushed her sock toy in through the crate opening and stood. "My grandmother had a farm. I remember the long hours she and my grandfather put in. A labor of love she always called it."

"Absolutely."

"How's Bullet doing?"

"He's going to be fine. One more night in the crate, I think, and we'll set him free."

"Does he mind being in here with the horses?"

"That kid thinks he's a horse. He's growing up underfoot, driving them crazy for attention, but they tolerate him." Javier chuckled. "But Adam is his favorite."

"They have a sweet bond, don't they?"

"Indeed. Adam stayed in the bunk room so he could be with him all night."

A boy and his dog. No, a very cute man and his dog. She definitely needed to walk. "I snuck a homemade toy in there for him when he wakes up. Thanks for letting me check on him."

"You're welcome anywhere on the farm, for as long as you like. Evening." Javier nodded.

She gave him a smile and went wandering through starlit paths and dreams with gorgeous new boots perfect for farm life. Javier's words traveled back to the cottage with her. How long did she want to stay? She was surrounded by stars, that was for sure. In the sky, under her feet and the people who shone around her.

I could get used to all this. But her plan was to regroup, heal, then get back to her life and her career. She'd do almost anything to get her career back, prove she could do it all again. Sneak into restaurants in disguise, taking every precaution to make sure no one recognized her. Eat out every night. Write until the wee hours of the morning to meet every deadline. Rise to one of the tops spots in the newspaper again. Again. Again. Again.

It was essential to who she was. And after how hard she'd worked, to lose it all like she had, shouldn't she do everything she could to reclaim it? But as she walked surrounded in glitter she wondered, did she really want a do-over? Or did she want something new?

Chapter Thirteen

Adam stopped short on the back porch of the main house. His heart didn't, though. It picked up and thudded, trying to make its way to Cassandra. She sat at the kitchen island, head tossed back in laughter. Sunlight flickered through her hair and caught her graceful neck. A notebook sat on the counter in front of her. Miranda and Katie were doubled over laughing, and Lily stood, hands on hips with a huge grin on her face.

Even from his spot on the porch he could see Elena roll her eyes. She swatted Lily on the hip with her towel then carefully pulled a tray of something scrumptious out of the oven. Pastries that bubbled and steamed. His stomach groaned. Great so now he was ornery, cranky *and* hungry.

He was *always* hungry. But ornery and cranky were two feelings Adam rarely entertained unless it came to the antiquated milking machine they'd buried this past spring. But it had been too long since he'd seen her, heard the lilt of her voice, held her hand, felt the softness of her long, elegant fingers calm in his hand. It hadn't been that long since he'd dreamed of kissing her, though. It rolled like an ongoing movie in his head. And imagining her in that shower, naked, with him...

He ran his hand over his eyes. She'd started the flirting, or had he? It didn't matter except that he didn't want to be a cheesy, annoying, creepy guy. Plus, he felt more like tipsy, drunk idiot. Neither one was a good appearance for any man.

He could partly blame the busy farm on their separation, but he was also conscious of her uncertainty, and he didn't want to overwhelm her with his desire. How crazy would it sound to tell her he'd fallen in love at first sight? *More specifically at first touch.*

Cruz walked by him and smacked his shoulder. "Going in to say hi or stand out here like a nitwit?"

Did he walk in, try to keep the drool from embarrassing the hell out of him? Or did he leave her in comfort? It could appear odd ogling her when she wasn't aware. But she sure was pretty to watch.

"View's not bad from here."

"True." Cruz got his own look of love-struck. And Adam felt marginally better about his own floppy heart...until his brother smirked at him and walked into the kitchen to kiss his wife.

Miranda set plates in front of Cassandra and Lily, who'd come to sit beside her. Something stronger dug into his heart. A pain, but a pain that was worth it. *Surrounded by his family. Welcomed. As though she belongs.* He wanted her to belong. And as desperate the need was to barge in and be a part of it all, to drown in her wildflower scent, he hesitated to break into this moment. Inside that kitchen, with her walls down, laughing and enjoying the company of his family belonged to Cassandra. It wasn't his to take.

Or maybe he was a fucking coward. One thing was certain, in addition to a dopey idiot, he smelled like he'd been rolling around in dirt and sweat all week and hadn't bothered to shower. No sense really turning her off with his stinky self.

Cassandra drew them in with a story. All eyes were on her, while she spoke with her hands in the air. And he couldn't hear a thing she was saying, but her smile danced with happiness.

Adam cemented the image to memory and left them enjoying their afternoon. There was still tons of work to be done to get crops harvested, hay brought in, the land and animals ready for winter. Adam smiled and took in his surroundings as he ticked off lists in his head. He added *take an evening walk with Cassandra Dorsey*.

Hope turned his day into high speed and kept him light on his feet. It was his new favorite emotion, especially when it came with images of the light on Cassandra's face.

The potato and cabbage fields were finally all harvested. One old tractor had bitten the dust no matter how much grease and labor Adam threw at it. So now grease was another layer of grime on his body.

"Come on, Bullet!" Adam yelled and his dog came running so fast down the hill he tripped and rolled at the end. Adam was beginning to think it was Bullet's favorite new trick.

"Time for our date."

Bullet quirked his head.

"I know we haven't asked her, but maybe if we get cleaned up, she'll take pity on us."

Pity wasn't exactly what he wanted, but a little wouldn't hurt, if it included her hands on him, her smile, and maybe she'd share some of her gorgeous laughter with him. Pity suddenly sounded amazing.

On the way to the Airstream, Bullet only got stuck once chasing the bees around a large patch of late dahlias.

"Hmm, not a bad idea, buddy. Not bad at all. We need all the assists we can get."

* * * *

Spending an entire morning being cooked for, and sampling new recipes for Brockman House Café, then an entire afternoon writing about it. The day couldn't get much better than that. What did they say about forming habits? Make them easy, accessible, enjoyable. An obsessed food lover-food writer could get used to this daily ritual fast. It was the perfect fuel. And even with all the words she'd furiously written down as the day passed, her mind still fed on more ideas. She'd already finished four essays.

Ideas raced through her head at an impossible speed. She could try to sell it as a column about places to go *from* San Francisco, small local farms and the connections they formed. The slow-food movement and farm-to-table had been done to death, but this place was inspiring. It was seduction at its purest form. Wonder, connection, belonging.

Even Adam, although absent from her presence the last few days, had continued his sweet and sexy texts every night, asking how she was doing, inquiring about her day. She'd missed that, people genuinely checking in for the sole purpose that they liked her and wanted to get to know her. Mmm, thinking of all the ways he'd hinted he wanted to get to know her flushed her entire body.

Adam: Bullet thanks you for his toy. It was awful nice of you to check in on him. I'm sorry I wasn't there to see you myself.

Cass: How is my favorite canine?

Adam: He does not make a good patient. How are you?

Cass: Good. I think there's something about the air in this place. A healing balm. I've been napping everyday as if my life depended on it. Sleep catch-up. Who knew how amazing it was? Thank you for the boots. They're lovely. You didn't need to do that.

She wasn't giving them back, though. She'd worn them every day. Already they felt like hers.

Adam: They made me think of you, beautiful, intriguing, full of stories. Stories I'd like to learn.

Oh, the man and his careful innuendo. Cassandra's heart fluttered to life every time a message came from him. *Well, it appears I've developed a crush.* Maybe it was the good kind of exhaustion from a wonderfully fulfilling day or the crisp and invigorating air surrounding her, but Cassandra decided she liked having a crush.

There was a knock at her door and Cass looked forward to opening it to whomever on this lovely farm it was. Of course her pulse sped up over who she wanted it to be. Still, she wasn't prepared for the sight in front of her.

Bathed in the early evening light was a proud pup, barely containing himself from jumping at her. His butt vibrated on the porch and he kept side-eyeing his human as if to ask how long he had to behave. A green bow tie graced his neck to match his new green sock bandage. His tongue hung out, his eyes sparkled — the cute thing was smiling.

His human was definitely smiling. A don't-you-dare-jump-on-her-you-crazy-mutt smile, which changed to heated lust as he snapped his gaze to Cass and sent hot licks climbing up her body.

"Cassandra…" His voice confessed all the things he wanted to do to her.

What? Tell me. Give me all the details. Although charming, his texts had left many things unsaid. Imagination was deliciously fun, but oh, now she wanted reality.

"Adam, Bullet." She found her own voice, hoarse and thready. If she invited him in right now, would they set the house on fire?

He held out a beautiful tin can bursting with more luscious purple dahlias. "Bullet and I wondered if you might like to take a walk with us. It's a pretty evening. Clear skies again, not too chilly.

She was far from chilly and barely refrained from whipping her sweater off. *Good thing it's not too heavy and hangs off one shoulder. Small concessions.* Would he notice if she plucked the flowers out and doused herself with the vase's water? She'd missed him. How could she have? She barely knew him, but he'd been on her mind all week.

"We missed you," he said. It calmed her racing heart to know his emotions echoed hers. She wished he really could read her mind. It would be easier than this awkward spitting the words out. "Texting is not the same as seeing you."

No, it definitely is not.

His puppy patience having worn out, Bullet grabbed a floppy, messy item, dropped it at her feet and barked for attention.

She knelt and let the tension release from her body. "You're looking pretty charming," she said to the dog, who smelled freshly bathed again. His toy did not.

"He loves the gift you gave him."

She laughed. "Does he expect me to touch it?"

"Bullet, come!" Adam called. "Nope, he carries it everywhere and plays with it himself. Sleeps with it. Drags it through all the disasters he gets into. I need to wash it, but the poor thing cried like the baby he is when I tried last night. I need to work on my distraction techniques. Sit, Bullet."

The dog plopped his butt down, but shimmers still ran through his body that was always itching to move.

It was a beautiful night and she did want to walk with this simple, kind, sexy man and his dog. *A treat, baby steps.* She could handle that.

Bullet, toy in his mouth, led the way prancing along, proud leader. She was startled out of her focus when Adam took her hand. Their fingers tangled together in different shades of colors connected.

"Pretty night, even prettier lady... Seems like the right thing to do, hold hands."

Right? The warmth of their connection traveled through her entire body. More like necessity, the end of longing. *Everything*. Which was a whole lot more complicated than baby steps.

Chapter Fourteen

"Where are you taking me, Adam Brockman?" They wove their way down a different path from the ones leading toward the barn where Bullet had slept, or the main house. She could hear the waves in the distance and realized she had yet to make it down the trailing path to the beach.

He squeezed her hand. "Where would you like me to take you, Cassandra?"

His arm rubbed the side of hers. Friction was delicious and all she could think of was what kind of friction their bodies could really make together.

She nudged him in the side. "You have all the smooth moves, don't you?"

He laughed and it broke the tension. "I have no moves whatsoever. I'm taking your lead."

"Now that's not true. Your innuendo and text moves are…" Cass fanned her face in embarrassment.

"Please do go on," he said, doing a valiant job of holding back his laughter this time. She could give him props. Every thought spilled out in her words and actions these days. Her filter and quiet patience lay behind her in smithereens. "I need all the confidence I can get with you."

"What do you mean 'with me'?" She appreciated that he didn't hold back either or talk in riddles. *Plain, open, honest, charming.* It was a balm to her cautious soul.

"This." He tapped her forehead as they made their way down to an open field. "A brilliant mind, tucked inside one seriously gorgeous body." His gaze brushed over her body again. "I know you have a kind heart, because you've taken care of my dog and don't hold grudges for being assaulted with cow poop."

It was her turn to laugh now. His words made her happy and lightheaded. She nearly tripped as they stepped off the path. Thanks to his grip, it was merely a tiny wrinkle in their walk. Even though her body flitted off kilter, when Adam twirled her back against the pretty long fence and wrapped his arms around her taking her lightheaded and woozy to a new level, his arms also centered her. It was definitely a new sensation in the crush department. She and Nate had met in college so long ago that Cass couldn't remember the lightheadedness. She'd liked him right away and they'd fallen into an easy, fun relationship. But this loss of sanity was colossal.

"But the most serious challenge," he said as he studied her face, "is whether or not I can dig through this faraway look of something serious or sad. What haunts you, Cassandra?"

Whoa. She had not expected that from him. Teasing, charming, all inuendoes aside, this man was sharper than she gave him credit for. His face was solemn and searching. She didn't want to expose all her damage, that she was a widow, that she was a lonely, directionless empty shell who'd recently got fired and had almost no friends left because she'd alienated them all. *Not yet.* She didn't want him to see her differently. *Not tonight.* So Cass fitted her arms around him, up under his jacket, gave him a nudge closer and dove in to the kiss she'd been fantasizing about all week in her waking hours and her dreams.

He was as still as a stone at first and she wondered if he'd pull away. But oh, she hoped he didn't. His lips were softer than she'd imagined. Even if this were a mistake, if he pulled away, she knew she'd remember that touch forever. *Please, please kiss me back.* Cass was nearly ready to plead before she ended things herself.

A gear kicked into place and all softness disappeared. He gripped her hips to hold her, as if she'd run away *now*, took a deep breath like he was breathing in all that was her and brought his A-game to the most intense kiss of her life.

"Cassandra, you slay me," he said roughly as he angled his head and savored her mouth as though it was the best meal he'd ever indulged in. She feasted back, but holy wow it was like he took control and lassoed her in, claiming, leading. He was a barely leashed animal vibrating under her fingers. Her hands fell from his back and she braced herself against the fence. *Yes,* she wanted to yell. *Do what you will with me.*

When she moved, so did he, gripping her face with his hands, capturing her body with his while he kissed her. Even his fingers shook, but that did nothing to mar the way he held her, preciously, running his thumbs over her cheekbones, kneading her neck while his lips journeyed. He made an expedition of her mouth. A completely satisfying and successful one, each nip and deep caress scoring straight into her blood, zinging lower and sharpening in her core. Pressed up against the fence, she clung to it for purchase and so she wouldn't jump him. She'd already angled into his body, his heat and the coursing want he exhibited for her. The perfect combination luring her as he rubbed his hips into hers, tangled their tongues together, stroked her skin to fervor. And she'd believed this day couldn't get any better. *Silly, silly fool.*

Then he stopped. Her eyes were closed in a dream. A dream she was jarred out of way too soon. Riled up and gasping for breath, she was too afraid to open her eyes. But Adam peeled her hands off the fence and linked their fingers.

"You're shaking." His gruff voice was that of a man who'd gotten completely carried away with her. But she didn't hear regret. His face mirrored her emotions. *Holy hell, that was intense and I want to do it over again.* But concern also reflected back at her.

"I think we were both shaking. It was pretty earth shattering. I was merely holding on." *For dear life.*

"Mmm." He quirked one side of his mouth up in that knowing, sexy smile of his that was full of secrets. "It's probably a good thing I stopped." He leaned in and kissed her neck. "We have a visitor."

"What?" Cass spun out of his arms.

"It's only Gracie." He was laughing at her again. She was being ridiculous, but having someone walk up while she was orbiting another dimension in Adam-Brockman-kiss-land would have been a bit embarrassing.

He unlatched the gate and invited her in. Cass took his hand, calming her stuttering breath, and marveled at this beautiful creature from up close.

At the sound of her name, the midnight-colored mare tossed her head around gracefully, almost preening. She whinnied at Adam, basking at his attention. Then she stilled herself, very carefully stepped closer to Cass, and leaned her forehead right against Cass'. The horse nuzzled and hummed, conveying her very heart right into Cass.

Cass sucked in a breath and closed her eyes. Gently putting her hands on either side of the majestic head, she held on and let out the breath she'd been holding, not just of that moment but the breath she'd been holding in since Nathan's death. With it, again, came the tears. Well, what could she do? She obviously had no control over them lately. *Guess the purging isn't completely finished.*

"Don't mind me. So many things, beautiful and sad make me cry these days."

"If something nudges your soul and brings you to tears, you shouldn't deny it," he offered, stroking Gracie's neck and running his fingers through Cass'. He must have ached with the need to touch her as much as she longed for him. And wow did she like his fingers in hers.

"Hmm." She rested against the massive, beautiful horse and let the beast absorb her tears. "Says the big, bold farmer who's probably never cried."

"You'd be surprised. I cried when my brothers went off to college. I cry every time a new horse is born. I won't even tell you how many tears I shed when we have to put one down. I'm not just a big dumb farmer," he teased her gently.

"Not dumb at all." Now she was blushing *and* crying. "I meant masculine, macho. Ignore me. I swear I'm not this much of a word idiot."

"I don't think you're any kind of idiot," Adam said.

"You're awfully forgiving. I haven't exactly been the epitome of intelligence or kindness since I met you. Snappish, dog-stealing, mixed-signal giver."

"Mmm," Adam said and made his way around his horse. He said it like he had a smile in his voice, like he enjoyed their confusing encounters so far. *Strange man.*

"I wouldn't call that kiss mixed signals."

Cass nuzzled Gracie, hoping to hide the shiver of desire that flitted through her.

"Was it?" He was standing next to her again. So close that again she felt compelled to lean into him, which was exactly why she didn't.

"No." *Not mixed, exactly. How much I wanted to keep going, keep exploring. And also everything in my past that makes the waters around me so, so murky for someone so kind and innocent as you.* Innocent? Was that really how she saw him. Younger, happy, carefree for sure, but that kiss... She was still simmering from the reaches of its heat.

"A question in your answer again. Does it have to do with your burdens?"

"In a way." Cass took in the lovely evening light as it settled things into deeper color around them. "Can we... Would it be okay to keep this moment about us, simple for now? It's too pretty and special to mar."

Without hesitation, Adam nodded and gave her that gorgeous full-mouth smile again. Even his eyes were full of happiness.

"Gracie's a pretty name for a pretty girl."

"She was a shell of herself when she came to me. She'd been wandering from place to place until I bought her. And she hadn't been treated well. Her coat was dull, she shied away, but I cared for her and with lots of patience she healed. When her light came back, I could see how graceful and sleek she was. At a quick glance she's fierce and dark, but when she blooms she's full of joy. She was my Gracie and the first time I called her that she tossed her head and pranced. She was happy, settled. It fit her."

"Your voice does that to a lady, calls her attention, settles in." She wanted to get back to the light flirting.

"Is that all it does?"

No. They weren't touching, unfortunately, but his voice traveled over her like an invitation. Unable to find her own words suddenly, her mouth parched, all she could do was shake her head.

Chapter Fifteen

Adam closed the distance. "Can I kiss you again?"

Another nod. Had he turned her speechless? He understood. He was completely unprepared for conversation at this moment.

Her eyes sparked at his approach, at him resting his hand on her hip, claiming back his favorite spot on her body. *I bet she has many, many spots I'd love to call my favorite.*

"Please," she said. *Not completely speechless, then*, and thank goodness, because her voice was now his favorite song on the wind, a lifeline he'd never known he needed. He tugged her head gently forward, running his fingers through her soft hair and searing their mouths together once more.

This time she didn't brace against the fence at her back from the storm that raced through them. This time she stood freely, and he was grateful because she used those long, graceful fingers to explore his chest.

She tasted of life and adventure, spices and sugar. "Spicy, sweet Cassandra."

"No one's ever called me sweet before," she said before she joined their mouths again.

"Delicious, sugar and cinnamon and orange." He dipped his lips to her neck, her cheeks before fumbling back to her mouth. Adam had kissed before, but talking while kissing, teasing and flirting with each was an aphrodisiac.

She arched into him fitting her hips to his. *Where they fucking belong.* That thought sawed at the last threads of control. Her soft, lush chest pressed up against him, their thighs rubbing against each other. Fuck, even with clothes in their way, his blood, his limbs throbbed with her power rushing between them. Now he wished for the fence at her back. He wanted to walk her up against it and ravage her right there. To have his mate in the wild green pasture under the evening sky and the hint of breeze whispering and teasing, their joined heat swirling around them.

Adam's blood led him as he took a step into her and she followed with one back. Another and another, their bodies dancing the same dance until Gracie's whinny and stomping hooves jarred them apart. Cass stared open-mouthed in shock. Her face was wild and alive with flushed cheeks and desire and a gaze that said *what in the ever-loving hell was that?*

"*That* was incredible," he said.

Again, she simply nodded, then bent over to catch her breath, and Adam laughed out his own winded frustration and tried to calm the boiling need inside.

"Good thing you interrupted us, Gracie." Adam ruffled her mane, but she sidestepped, seeking attention, showing off for Cassandra. Cass recovered from their explosion, or at least did an amazing job of pretending, and interacted with his horse. He couldn't take his eyes off the woman.

Gracie nudged his head. "Hungry, are you?" *Fucking hunger. Have I been starved my entire life?* Now he'd had a taste of Cass and he wondered if he'd ever be full. It scored through his heart. A branding that settled in his soul, one more piece of his life clicking into place. *The most important part,* his heart whispered.

"Shall we feed her?" Cass asked.

"Mmm." He was still stuck on studying her, learning her, when Gracie swatted him with her tail. "All right, girl. If we don't, she'll get ornery."

"You." Cass soothed his horse. "I don't believe you'd get ornery for a second."

"Ha!" Adam exclaimed. "Hunger and boredom both get her riled up. If she doesn't eat or get to run like the wind, she pesters us nonstop."

"As any girl would." She ran her fingers through Gracie's mane. "I'd love to ride her sometime. Could I?" With her asking softly like that, her face flushed and eyes excited, he'd give her anything she requested. Gracie sped up her dance, nodding, and they both laughed.

"I think she understands you," Adam said. "You can ride her whenever you want." *I can't wait to see you on my horse.* His two beauties flying across the land, uninhibited, wild. He wasn't sure if it momentarily settled his hunger or stirred it to think of her as his, but life as he'd known it before had been altered in a pasture during a few moments of kissing. *Lifechanging, electrifying moments.* A tidy package all tied up had been ripped open and a whole new world awaited him. It was a strange and heady knowledge and he carried it with him. Hand in hand, he and Cassandra strolled Gracie back to the barn for the night. He gave a whistle and Bullet bounded out of the trees to follow.

Their hands linked, Cass walked nearly aligned with his body. Each touch of their legs, each brush of their arms stoked his need for her, for more, for everything with her.

"I think I like you, Adam."

"You think?" He choked out the words followed by laughter, at himself most likely. He was the dope in this scenario. While he'd been mentally sketching out their life together, she'd decided she maybe liked him. Whoa, boy did he have his work cut out for him.

She laughed too. And he squeezed her hand. "I sound like a kid passing notes in school, don't I?" Since their first awkward meeting she let her guard down, said whatever was on her mind. He grinned with the memory. There were many sides to this woman. Bold, intelligent, beautiful, tart, serious, easy, full of burdens, thoughtful. Adam learned more every day. "I just meant—" Her tone had taken on one of regret, all silliness gone.

"Oh." He got it now and took the kick to his gut. "How did I not see the 'but' coming."

"No, no, not...I don't...not like you're thinking. I mean...*blech*." She stopped as he led Gracie into her stall and filled her bucket with food. "It's a good *but*, I think."

"There you go with the innuendos this time." He couldn't help but grin. She was beautiful in the silhouette, the sun fading behind her and such a serious look on her face while she concentrated on getting her words exactly right.

"Stop flirting with me for one second so I can think." She held up her hand as if to block him even though they stood more than ten feet apart. *Ah, so you feel it too, the topsy-turvy world.*

"Promise. Can I flirt more when you're done?"

"Yes," she said immediately, and he breathed more easily knowing that all hope was not lost. Maybe it wasn't a bad *but* at all.

"I didn't come here, to Brockman Farms, for anything like this." She gestured between them. "In fact, I kind of ran away, needed to get away...to be alone and re-center myself in a way."

"Deal with your burdens?"

She nodded. "It's been a good thing, the time to think away from my life, interacting with your family, wonderful, delicious naps. I've been writing. You." Her entire face brightened with her smile when she said that last word. "I need to go slow."

He said goodnight to his horse, closed the barn and, linking their fingers again, walked Cassandra back to her cottage. *If slow means a lifetime with you, then sign me up.* All these emotions rushed from his heart to his head. He wanted to blurt his words out, but she needed careful and cautious. He could give her both.

"You like me." He quirked his mouth at her. "But you want to be careful, not get swept away in this awesomeness?" Like he already was. How was he still standing upright? Perhaps his new world had centered around him already, in the span of a few seconds, as he came to know his future would be linked with hers.

"I...I—"

"Jesus." His stomach sank. "You look like you're going to faint again." They'd reached her cottage where she sat abruptly on the stairs and put her head in her hands. "Are you okay? I didn't mean to freak you out." Shit, he'd done exactly what he was trying to avoid. He'd been teasing, but something serious was going on in her head.

She took his hand and pulled him down next to her. "I don't think I'm going to faint. I... It's hard to talk about." Cass took a deep breath and in the span of a few silent seconds Adam thought *he* might faint. "I was married. Once. It feels like it was from a different dimension completely. Especially these last few months. Some days it's stark and clear in my mind. Others it's strange and difficult to remember."

He tried not to display his shock, but sat quietly and listened. Bullet padded over and cuddled up next to Cassandra with his soft puppy head resting next to her leg.

"Nathan. He was killed by a drunk driver seventeen months ago, almost eighteen now."

"Cassandra, I'm sorry." She wasn't carrying regular-sized burdens. Most people would be crushed under her boulders.

"It was awful. Ha." Her laugh was sharp and bitter. "I mean that's putting it mildly, isn't it? Afterward, a lot happened. I lost my dream job. My sense of smell deserted me, and I couldn't be a food writer without being able to truly enjoy, or hate, for that matter, the food I was reviewing. My boss had me writing about other things for a while, but that didn't work out. I've been sort of dead inside for a long time, until the last few months. Well..." She paused, ruffled Bullet's fur and turned to him with wet eyes. "I'm so sorry I ruined our beautiful walk."

"No." Adam forced out the words that wanted to strangle his throat. "I'm grateful you shared with me. I want to know about your life, your scars as well as your dreams. I…I don't have the right words. You survived a trauma I suspect many wouldn't be able to recover from."

"I wasn't sure I would for a while. Fortunately, and believe me there were moments when I thought unfortunately, life keeps going and we keep moving forward. I've been writing about food again, since I arrived here. So much." She tangled their fingers together and he watched the color and happiness breathe back into her features. "My sense of smell came barreling back when a handsome farmer threw manure on me."

Adam threw his head back and groaned. Tension eased out of him. "The fairies were laughing that day for sure." It was her gentle smile at his silly words that lessened the rest of his shock. He wanted to haul her into his lap and comfort her, then kiss her until no more burdens remained.

Bullet had fallen asleep in a pile of fur and limbs and his snores gave them both a chuckle.

"I do like you, a lot," she whispered. He brought his focus back to her. *Serious but calm expression on her face. Wide-eyed, caution gone.* God she was beautiful. He could easily daydream in those eyes of hers forever. "I also want to be careful." She rubbed her chest. Adam took her hand back and kissed it. They sat under the starlight in silence, the air cradling their emotions between them. When he stood, he tugged her up with him.

Adam wrapped his arms around her. "I promise to be careful with you, Cassandra Dorsey."

"I squished our lovely evening."

Adam shook his head. He gave her a gentle kiss. "You didn't."

"You're sure?"

Adam lifted his mutt into his arms. "I can't believe I'm carrying you home again, you sleep monster."

Before he headed down the path he said, "That was the best first date I've ever had, Cassandra. Sleep well."

"Goodnight, Adam," she called through the crisp night air.

A heaviness settled in Adam's chest on his walk home and it had nothing to do with the weight of his dog asleep in his arms. The cute mutt had had a good date too.

But what were his worries compared to the weight of her burdens? Jesus, married, *widowed?* How had she survived so much and come out so powerful and strong? It was one more hint of her depths and he was honored she'd told him.

But his mind wouldn't settle. Her heart had belonged to someone else. Could a person give their heart again? He'd believed he'd only ever give his to one woman. The question that haunted him during his sleepless night was *can I compete with a ghost?*

Chapter Sixteen

It was freeing to walk up the hill to Brockman House and walk right into the kitchen as herself, hair in a messy ponytail, no makeup on, save for a bit of lip gloss. The familiarity made her smile, hearing the ladies before she entered, breathing in the amazing aromas already simmering on the stove. Her mind buzzed with new essay ideas.

"Hi, Cass," Miranda called.

But today it wasn't the baked goods that snagged her attention at first. *Now those are some good genes.* She'd met each of the brothers, but the three of them standing side by side, well, it was downright unfair to the rest of the male population. Tall and sexy, and unbelievably fit from hard daily labor. The force from their grins nearly blinded her. Although the youngest, Adam was nearly half a foot taller than both his brothers, and wider too. All those muscles she wanted to learn about on an intimate basis. Goodness, it made her shiver.

"Yeah, good morning, Cass," Turner drawled and not-so-subtly elbowed Adam.

"Boys," she tossed back. He wasn't the only one who could tease. And they did look boyish today. Especially Adam in his old T-shirt, worn jeans and a baseball hat that had seen better days two decades ago. He wore it backward and when he smiled at her, she was struck with the knowledge that he was happy. It surrounded him. They all were. His mouth...*mmm*, that mouth ignited her dreams. But even it was powerless against the food amazingness seducing her senses.

"Wow!" Cass gazed in reverence. Setting her bag down, she nearly drooled over the pan as the steam hit her in the face. *Best spa treatment ever. Cinnamon roll facial.*

"Yeah," Miranda sighed as she put one on a plate for Cass. "I think this was when I first fell in love here."

"Yeah, with me, gorgeous," Cruz said.

"No, honey, with Elena."

The brothers burst out laughing.

Cass tried to camouflage her drooling sigh. *I could play that sound on repeat all day.*

Miranda held up half of her gooey roll. "Can you blame me?"

The rolls were hypnotic. All three men followed the path of Miranda's knife as she separated the caramelized, puffy, perfection. They were snagged and in mouths faster than Cass could yell, "Interception!" She must have been gawking because Adam asked, "You going to eat yours, Cassandra?" He said her name as if it were an invitation to sin.

"Now, there's a way to win her heart," Turner said. They were all staring at her. Was Adam supposed to win her heart? Did she want him to? But really they were all a bunch of hooligans — their gazes were centered on her plate.

"Some things are more important than love," Adam said solemnly before he reached his long, tan, muscled arm out, snagged her cinnamon roll and took off jogging out through the back door. He turned once to give her a wink before he was gone, leaving Cruz and Turner standing stunned in the kitchen.

"He... I... Wait," Turner sputtered. "Dammit, he got the last one again. How the hell does he do it? Every single time."

"Bastard. He's got skills," Cruz said in awe as he studied his own empty plate.

They weren't the least bit sorry that she was the one who'd had her pastry stolen, which made Cassandra laugh. Adam had done it for that reason, she suspected, to lighten the mood, let her off the hook from the win-her-heart comment.

"Well, it's a good thing for you poor souls that I have another tray right here," Miranda said. "Now get out of the kitchen unless you're going to help. Too much of a distraction."

"You could open a café with these." Cass leaned into the new tray. "Damn, sugar, cinnamon, caramelized nuts. Someone knew what they were doing when they put that combination together."

"Did I miss all the good stuff?" Lily flew into the kitchen and, even in her work clothes and with her hair pulled back under a hat, exploded with beauty and confidence.

Cass hummed. "You didn't miss these. I might need another, or ten."

"Not those." Lily sighed like they were all four-year-olds and she needed to speak very slowly. "Did I miss all the talk about your date with Adam last night?"

Choking on the best cinnamon rolls in the universe was not an act Cass wanted to add to her skills.

"I'm so sorry!" Lily patted her back gently.

"Maybe you're not meant to have one of these today." Miranda laughed.

"Hopefully third time's a charm," Cass said, sipping her creamy coffee to soothe her throat. *Coffee tastes really weird to me today.* She pushed the cup back. *At least I can smell it again.* She pushed it even farther away. *Not smelling so great either.*

"Third time?" Lily snagged two rolls for herself and sat down.

"Adam stole her first one," Miranda said.

"That jerk!" Lily grumbled. "I never did like that whole 'boys tease the girls they like' thing. Stealing one of these babies is an act of war in my mind. I'll help you tackle him in the manure later." Lily attempted to devour a roll in one bite.

Cass laughed. "I think I've had enough manure to last me a while."

"Speaking of babies." Miranda raised her eyebrow at Lily. "Something you want to tell us, eating for two these days?"

"Nope," Lily said with a smug smile on her face. "But not for lack of trying." Which had them all howling.

"Come on now, get to the good stuff. You, Adam, first date?" Lily drank her own coffee like it was the source of all life and pushed Cass' mug back toward her.

"I don't think I can do coffee today." She studied her mug like it was an alien. "Are there tiny hidden elves spreading the word that I went for a lovely walk with Adam last night?"

"Ha! I knew it! Turner was in the barn office last night when you guys put Gracie in. He said you were just talking, but I know better. There's no *just* anything with these men. They lure you in with their handsomeness and crooked all-knowing smiles and spin you around until you can't stand up straight unless you give in and give your heart over. The only thing that makes it okay is you get their heart in return."

By the end of her whirlwind, Lily was sighing with hearts in her eyes. Cass' fear must had shown on her face. Miranda set a glass of water in front of her and patted her hand. "Lily, I think you've scared her silent. You don't have to share anything with us you don't want to."

Cassandra gulped the cool water. A hot flash washed over her compounded by exhaustion, but she wondered if maybe some of that tired came from spending months being cooped up silent and lonely. "I'm not sure I have a heart to give to anyone, especially someone as special as Adam," she admitted.

"*Pish*, everyone has a heart. We'll help you dig yours out if necessary. We can handle anything—past relationships gone bad, trust issues, fear of commitment… And if we can't, between Miranda, Elena and I, we have plenty of romance novels that can guide us, or at least give us a good, sexy story."

Cass smiled. These women were all in with their friendship, which was lovely. "It might be more difficult than what you're imagining, because I think I buried it when I buried my husband," she said quietly.

"What?" Miranda covered her mouth and now looked like *she* was the one who was going to puke.

"Oh, Cass." Lily set her second cinnamon roll down. "No, I'm so sorry. Gah, you'll be hearing that a lot from me if I keep shoving my boot down my throat. Here I am making light of your pain. Please excuse me."

"You didn't know. And I...I like your teasing and lightheartedness. It's wonderful to laugh and joke about handsome men with friends. It reminds me that there is a happier, lighter side to life. I haven't really felt fully alive again until I came here. It's just...well...I sense Adam is one special heart and mine is..." She flailed, searching for the right words. "Sad, buried, scared?" She sure didn't want it to be. "I don't know anymore."

"I can't speak from your perspective, but I do know loss. And I think we can love someone when they die, but that doesn't mean that's all the love we have or that our hearts aren't replenishable. And Brockman Farms is not a bad place to find that love again, especially with someone like Adam."

Cass closed her eyes and sighed. She so wanted to believe Lily was right, because as broken as she'd been when Nathan died, she didn't want to be alone or lonely forever. She wanted love again.

"Lily," Miranda said.

"I can't help it. She's awesome and I already don't want to lose this friendship we have with her. And the way Adam is when he talks about her, gazes at her. He's always had one focus, the farm."

"True, but we can't know what it's like to lose Cruz or Turner. It's her heart, honey."

Lily paused and all the color drained from her face. "You're right. I'd be nothing, a hollow shell full of emptiness and—"

Cass took pity on her new passionate friend. "I was that for sure. In the beginning for months. And I was angry, so fucking angry at him, as if it were his fault. I lost my sense of smell, my desire for food. Which sucked because that is, *was* my career. It was devastating. After anger, I was lost and numb for a long time. Then angry again because I wanted to *feel* anything. I was pretty stupid for a few months this summer, going to stupid bars, with stupid men, dragging along my stupid dead heart.

"Partly why I came here was to find peace. I'm writing, I'm hungry, I can smell. There is definitely something special about this place, but Adam deserves someone who can give him everything And I'm determined to get my career back as *The San Francisco Chronicle*." Could she have both a new love and her career?

"Holy crap! Wait, you're Ms. Financier! I used to read your column religiously. Then you disappeared. I always felt like I was eating at those restaurants even when I wasn't. Holy tomatoes, that time you eviscerated the head chef at that tapas restaurant when he berated his female dishwasher and you overheard. You're one of my heroes!"

Cass smiled. "Wow, I'd forgotten about that dinner. Definitely didn't write much about the food."

"I always loved that about your column, though, the times when you infused the restaurant review with hints of the personal." Lily's eyes flashed wide. "Crap, I'm going to be late." She jumped off her stool, hugged Cass tightly, threw her arms around Miranda and rushed by Elena on her way back into the kitchen.

"Is she always so…"

"Like a mini-tornado?" Miranda laughed. "No, but when she's taking a break from work, she's like a worker bee rushing everywhere, soaking up as much of life as she can. She means well, about the love and hearts and all."

"I can tell that about her from yards away. She glows with happiness and wants everyone around her to be as happy. I guess I'm just trying to take baby steps to get my happy back in the heart department. Having it crushed to smithereens is a difficult experience to get over."

"I can't even imagine, Cass. But I don't think there's any rule book or scoreboard that says you don't get to find happiness again. I think it's the opposite. I think we shove judgment and self-doubt and fear out of the way and try to fly again, scary as that all sounds."

Cass let Miranda's words take root. "You'd like my sister-in-law. She's been trying to tell me the same thing. It's an unexpected treasure in coming here, all of you, this friendship, the warmth, the way you've opened yourselves up to me."

"Well, you know we're practicing our hospitality on you for when the café and barn dinners start, right?" Miranda winked taking them out of the serious.

"I don't think you need any practice."

"If you're as good a writer as Lily says, you might not need much either to get your mojo back."

"A girl can dream, can't she?" Cass smiled and while Miranda studied lists for the new café whose opening Cass couldn't wait for, for her new friends' sake and her own, she jotted notes and imagined soaring through life again as opposed to it beating her down. And she imagined how she and Adam could fly together. A burst of hope blossomed inside her.

Giddiness and warmth and anticipation all woven together.

Chapter Seventeen

"You stole my cinnamon roll."

Ahh her voice. Adam's entire body ignited with it. His heart perked up, started its gallop, and his blood thrummed with awareness. All his senses beat her name. *Cassandra.* She was so dang pretty, pretending to pout, but fierce and powerful all the same, and all untangled this afternoon. Her hair was loose, long wavy locks flying in the breeze. Vibrant eyes, *happy eyes.* He climbed down from the fence, tossed his gloves to the side and wasted no time at all in stalking her and wrapping his arms around her. He didn't kiss her even though it was all that dragged his mind these days, especially with their bodies pressed together. A little flirting was his intention. If it happened to lead to kissing, he'd know he was doing it right.

"All bets are off when it comes to those cinnamon rolls." He leaned in and dragged his lips, his nose up her neck. "Decadent, with all that sugary caramelized goodness, unique places with hints of spices I can't name." He did kiss her then, behind the ear, lingering as the heat built around them.

"Cardamom," she breathed. "And orange."

"Never would have guessed. I need you to lead me." Adam brushed his finger over her full mouth. "All these hidden secrets I'm in search of."

"I don't know if you want all my secrets."

She wasn't pushing him away or pulling back. *Progress.* "I'm pretty sure I do. Like this one here. Let me guess." He gently kissed the corner of her mouth then narrowed his eyes at her. "Didn't know powdered sugar was on those glorious rolls."

She laughed as if she'd succeeded in tricking him. And he frowned when she wiped her mouth. "Didn't know I got sugar on me."

On you? You're all the sugar and spices wrapped up in the perfect package for me.

"It's from the donuts that came later."

He squeezed her to him and moaned. "I missed donuts?"

"Brought you some." She handed him a small brown paper bag and when he opened it, he nearly fainted in pleasure.

"I bow to those women," Adam said after inhaling one of the donut holes, still warm, with sugary goodness melting on the outside.

"You bow, huh? Guess who made them?" She pointed to herself and his smile stretched across his face. "I had a chance to take a class years ago when I was in Portugal. *Sonhos,* they're called. Dreams."

He gave her a loud, smacking, powdered-sugar-covered kiss and twirled her around, which made her laugh again. Every time she let loose with that beautiful sound, he noticed nuances of it. *A spring tree in bloom letting all her bright foliage show, from light green to grassy, growing into a darker hue with certainty.* He was going to spend a lifetime making her laugh. "I'll promise you anything if you make those for me again."

"Maybe you don't have to beg. Maybe I'd like cooking for you." Cassandra untangled herself as she said it. Christ, the woman could tease. Telling him she wanted to cook for him while separating them. And this time it was her turn to leave him standing behind.

"I need to do some work." Her smile was all happiness and light.

"Now?" He glanced from the food of his dreams to the woman of his dreams.

"A little bit." Was she taking pity on him?

"Are we walking again tonight, Cassandra?"

"I'd like that."

* * * *

The promise of an evening walk with his lovely lady had Adam rushing through his end-of-day chores and singing in the shower. He was focused solely on getting to her, seeing her, touching her. Maybe they'd walk down to the shore and feel the spray of water from the waves. Maybe she'd be chilly enough to lean into him, let him wrap his arms around her. *Fuck!* All rational thought of walking and wooing left him in a breath.

"Hi," she said in a dry voice. Her hair a mess, her face was dreamy sleepy. She wore matching cream-colored sweats that were made out of some soft fabric, giving her entire aura a glow. She gave a huge yawn, covered her mouth and giggled.

Shit. I'm done for. He braced himself against the doorway before the force of her knocked him down. "Did I wake you?"

She nodded and smiled. "I told you this place keeps luring me into the best naps. Sleep has become my favorite thing to do." Goofy smile on her face, Cass scrunched up her shoulders and wrapped herself in a hug. "Oh, I forgot our walk." If this was how she looked every time she woke up, and he was with her, they'd never make it out of bed. She was even cuter when she pouted sleepily. "No Bullet?"

"I left him snoring at home. Kid had an eventful day."

"Another one? Is he okay?" She took his hand and rubbed her graceful thumb over his knuckles. That fire in his belly that had been there since he'd walked away from her in frustration that first day itched to burn faster, hotter. And it was getting harder and harder not to take over and touch every part of her. Even the cold wind that had blown in couldn't dampen the way he burned for her.

"He's fine. A little horse chase is all." Adam cleared his throat and watched their hands.

"Adam?"

"Huh?" He caught her gaze. Was her expression always this open or only when she was still in the last flights of dreams and sleep? Deep brown eyes, clear and honest gazed at him questioning, searching.

"I don't want to walk." She wanted to take her time, and he'd give her anything she wanted, but the words flew out like the breath he'd been holding in anticipation.

A link clicked inside her, or maybe she mindread his pure unadulterated lust. In answer, she took his other hand with hers and walked him into her cottage. Cass carefully took his jacket off and hung it by the door while Adam kicked off his boots. She brought her hands to his collar and teased the skin of his neck. Slowly she ran her fingers over his chest, admiring him with all that hot hunger in her eyes all without saying a word. Gone was the sleepy goofball. The desire flickering in her expression mirrored what beat inside him.

He didn't hold back then. He kissed her and, thank God, he wasn't as fucking uncoordinated as a colt, although he was still unwound. More than unwound. This was Cassandra, and everything with her was more intense, richer, deeper, including the way she shimmied her body against his.

He walked them into the living room and stumbled before making it safely to the sofa. "It's all I can think about, kissing you."

"Me too," she whispered in his ear as he sampled her neck. He reached his hands under her sweater, sweatshirt whatever the hell it was. Those words threatened to slice the thread of his patience. If he could just make them one, skin to skin, perhaps it would bank his desire, give him time to think. Fuck, he'd lost all rationality.

"This okay?"

"Wonderful," she sighed as skin met skin, and arched like a flower opening in search of more sunshine.

"This is even better." Cass climbed onto his lap and straddled him Their kissing turned wild and messy and sloppy as they devoured each other, like it was a race to see who could find the best morsel. He held her to him with his hands on the smooth, warm skin of her back, and she ground against him. "Oh, yes," she sighed.

His hands found their way underneath the lip of her sweatpants and he grabbed her lush ass and tugged her even closer. He rubbed his hands over her soft skin, teased his thumb between her luscious globes.

"Yes, that." She writhed against him, unabashedly unshy in how she moved her sexy body. "Your hands on me there…"

"Cassandra." He chased her mouth again and when she arched back, he used one hand to drag her sweater off and bury his head in her neck, roving lower, tasting and licking and scenting her. He continued his caress on her behind, then snaked his touch around to palm her chest through her tank top, dreaming of exploring all of her. "You're so warm and soft…"

Fuck he wanted to explode out of his jeans from the torture as she moved against his hard cock. Even with all their clothes between them, the simmering heat promised to burn. Layers of fabric added to the friction.

"Jesus, Adam, you're going to make me come. It's been so long…I…"

He wanted that and more. "Come for me, Cass. I've got you." He wanted to watch her lose control while she came, but his ache to be connected took over and he claimed her mouth again.

Honey. She tasted of honey and hidden gems that he might never discover, which didn't mean he'd ever quit searching. It only meant a lifetime of precious investigation in the form of the most amazing kisses of his life. *Only.* Such a sad word for that possibility. *All* was more like it. But even that was too narrow in scope. *Infinite, universe, forever.* He was getting closer. Maybe there was no word yet invented to encompass how he felt at the chance of a life with Cassandra Dorsey.

Hard nipples pebbled for him as he rubbed and caressed them between his fingers. He devoured her lips one last time and she broke in a burst of firelight during the darkest night. Her body came apart over his and he captured her, holding her, savoring every movement, every scream and sigh.

Then all he could hear was their mutual breathing like they'd run a sprint, chased each other to the finish line. *Best fucking run of my life.* He held her slumped against him and whispered soothing words into her ear while he smoothed his hand over her back in a gentle warmth. The whispered words were as much for his benefit as hers if he was going to not embarrass the hell out of himself. He was already in a constant state of hard around her, heck, even *thinking* about her, but it was all nothing compared to right now, his body coiled and ready to burst. "I've got you. Cass, that was incredible."

Her head shook on his chest back and forth and he captured her scent as her hair tickled his nose.

"No?"

"You are incredible," Cass said, lifting her head and offering him a dopey smile and flushed skin, and poking his chest before she collapsed back onto him. When he laughed, he could feel that too, beating into her and resonating back against his own body. To laugh with someone like this after something so intimate. *Fuck!* Adam tightened his arms for a minute and choked back his emotion. Intimacy was a thing that had been missing from his life for a long time. Perhaps since childhood. Now that he'd found it, it occurred to him it was the most precious gift he'd ever been given, and he only hoped he was strong enough to cherish it.

Chapter Eighteen

It took a few minutes for Cassandra to feel the weight of her own limbs again as the sensation of flying drifted away and she came back into herself. Flying felt amazing. *He smells good. That was fantastic.* Even her thoughts jumbled together competing for attention. *More than fantastic. I think I left the planet for a few minutes.* And Adam Brockman was not only responsible for rocketing her into space—he'd caught her when she returned. He held her and murmured soft words that helped stitch the frayed parts of her back together.

Cass rubbed her cheek and hands over Adam's chest, expanding to his arms and neck. Returning to the present, eyes closed, she learned him. Nuances slipped into her conscious. The sexy, cologne of Adam Brockman's being. Soft, clean, flannel shirt, and even softer skin beneath it on his neck as she nuzzled. Strong, hard body and large roving hands doing things to her. Unimaginable, wonderful things. All sorts of places on her body still tingled.

Mmm, she wanted to curl up into him and arch around all at the same time. *Whoa!* He was still hard. She reached down to rub her hand over his jeans, to connect with all that pulsing heat. But then Adam linked her hands with his and pulled her arms away from his body.

"Cass." Her name was a plea.

If there was ever a time for whimpering, now was it.

Her body stiffened and she opened her eyes. "You don't want to?" Cass was suddenly shy or uncertain. Maybe it hadn't been as earthshattering for him. Duh! of course it hadn't been.

"Darlin'." Adam slumped his head against the back of the couch. When he pierced her with need and desire written all over his face, she let go of some of her tension. Especially because not only was he boasting a smile, but because his words were deep and raspy. The man sounded parched. "Want is *not* the issue. I've been wanting since the first time I touched you, felt your hips beneath my hands, breathed in your wild scent like you'd been rolling around in a field of flowers to taunt me."

Oh, she wasn't uncertain anymore. He'd whisked that away as if he'd stripped off all her clothes in one greedy swoop and dragged his hard, calloused fingers down her naked skin, staking his claim on her forever. Her body reacted as if he had and her core sought to be closer, to connect, her heat against his. Goodness gracious, the storm they'd create together.

"Darlin'," he groaned and held her hips steady, whipping her out of her hazy desires.

"You're back to *darlin'* me, Adam. Is that your way of patronizing?" she teased. "Trying to tell me what *I* do or do not want?"

"Hell no," he said. "I have many, many faults, but patronizing takes too much wasted energy." He was indeed not a man to waste energy. All open and honest and puppy-dog-like. Confidence oozed from him in his sexy swagger. He grabbed her top and carefully put it over her head. The fibers surrounded her, but it was no match for Adam's radiating heat. "You said you needed to take things slowly."

Ahh, not so silly now. Her poor battered heart barely remembered what that felt like, to be cared for, but it stirred in her, yawned and curled up like a cat under the sun and sighed out contentment. Cass closed her eyes and nodded, afraid that if she spoke, it would be in tears instead of words.

"I solemnly swear not to darlin' you anymore if it truly offends you." His easy tone made it safe for her to face him. "The *last* thing I want to do is offend." *Earnest, offering up whatever she needed, so young.* Lost in her dreamy cloud of interest in him, it struck her how his confidence and guile transferred into youth. *I don't even know how old he is.*

"I don't mind it," she said. "It's just...I'm so much older than you it feels silly. Doesn't it?"

"So much older?" he gasped. Then, using those miraculous hands, he quick-tackled her to the couch and found a vulnerable spot on her waist to stroke before he smacked her lips with his and sat up. "How old do you think I am?"

The laughter that bubbled out of her refreshed and rejuvenated, gave her power she'd buried along with her heart...until her brain clicked in again. "Twenty-two?" Her words sounded more strangled than she'd meant them. Had she really been making out with a twenty-two-year-old? Did it matter? *Yes,* her brain whispered, *because he has his entire life ahead of him and you've already lived yours. No!* her soul screamed back. *I'm nowhere near done living yet!* It felt good to stand up to bullies, especially internal ones. She had lived a life, and that life had been ripped out from under her. Now she had to choose, move forward or stay sinking. And she had no intention of being robbed of the potential of a second start.

He smacked his chest. "I'll have you know I'm the ripe old age of twenty-seven."

Cass melted back into the easy. He was so good-natured, so comfortable to be with, to tease. *Good-natured is the last thing he was when devouring my lips and body with his hands, giving me an orgasm extravaganza.* But he hadn't made things awkward at all. The man wasn't selfish. *Hot as hell. Charming. Kisses like the devil.* But it was this easy silliness she loved right now in this moment. It wrapped around her heart in strands, a foundation, safety, enjoyment.

"Good Lord," she sighed dramatically. "Practically an old man."

"Well?" he asked. Adam rubbed her hand in his, toyed with her palm.

"Well what, Grandpa?"

"Do I meet your age requirement for using terms of endearment like darlin'? Or would you prefer queen, goddess, badass?"

"Permission granted to change them out when the whim hits you," Cass said primly.

"Now, Ms. Cassandra," he drawled, mocking her impression of him as a swaggering cowboy full of hot air. "My vocabulary or age might not be as generous as yours, but—"

"Hey." She smacked him again. He laughed, dodged and nipped at her lips "Making fun of a woman's age will get you nowhere good. I'm thirty-five."

"Ahh." There was that lovely caress again on her palm. One of care, of listening, of learning, of possession. "So, older, wiser *and* prettier," he said.

"I'd say your word game is right on point, Adam Brockman," she said softly.

"Glad to know I've got something going for me."

"I see a man with many good qualities, no faults yet."

Adam grinned. "I'm afraid to tell you my faults. Now that I know more about you...you might end things right here."

She sat up and clasped their hands together. "Now you have to tell me."

His frown was so serious and solemn. *Oh shit, maybe it really is something bad. Now the truth comes out. He's got a side hustle of drugs or a wife stashed away somewhere. He is too good to be true.*

"I can't cook."

"You..." Cass blinked and wondered if she was still floating above the earth. The way he said it, as though he were in a closed confessional.

"Nothing, not at all. I'm horrible."

Cass burst out laughing. "You're joking."

"What idiot would joke about a thing like this?" Taking her hand with his, he clutched his chest. His heart still galloped under those luscious muscles of his. His expression tightened, so serious, so wounded, so scared. She immediately took pity on him.

"Are you hungry?"

"Always." There was that heady look in his eyes again when he answered, and she *knew*. She knew he meant for many, many things, not just food. *I feel the same*, she wanted to shout, to fling herself like a cheerleader in motion. So *not* the definition of taking things slow. And, lovely though it was of him to care for her, she needed to take care of her own heart. And slow was good. Slow was wonderful, if this was his version. Mmm, slow could give a lady a chance to catch up.

"Well." She took his hand, pulled him up and led him to the kitchen. "Sit." Cass pointed to the stools. "Let's start with dinner, shall we?"

"As long as that's only the beginning." A slow, sexy grin spread across his face and she nearly had to wave her hand in front of her face to cool the simmer down again.

Chapter Nineteen

All the work in the world could wait for once. Farm tasks would always be there and he would always get things done, but sharing his news with Cass came before the farm today. Sharing it with her via text or even words wouldn't be nearly enough, he wanted to show her. And now, on this late fall afternoon while the deep blue sky beamed across his land, was the perfect moment.

Adam: Interested in a ride?

Cass fired back *Yes*, with heart-eye emojis. Emojis had been foreign before she had come into his life.

And now she was here. *Everything. She's everything.*

There it was again the sprinting of his heart when she walked into his sight in the barn. She'd woven her hair into a braid and her smile brightened the path before her.

"Cass," he croaked out. She stole his breath and tied him in knots.

"Hi," she said. He held out his hand and it was only then with her touch that his heart settled, no longer lost and needy but vibrating with being found by the other part of his soul.

"How was your morning?"

"So good," she squealed. "I helped make bread and I finished two essays." She practically danced around him. It warmed him to know this place gave her that. Hopefully he was a part of that happiness. He wanted her to love it here the way he did, but he knew a forced love wouldn't last. He'd witnessed that kind of relationship growing up and wanted nothing to do with it. She leaned into his chest and took a deep breath. Forever with her was his goal. "You smell better than freshly baked bread. How do you do that?" A laugh boomed out of him and kicked his worries away.

"I smell like horse and barn and hay."

"Mmm." Her muffled voice rumbled against his chest. "Sexy farmer." She grinned. "That's what I'm going to name it. I'm going to bottle it and spread it over my sheets so I can have it in my dreams, pour it over me in the shower so it surrounds me in steam when I think of you."

Adam walked her right back into the stall and didn't stop until she was up against the boards. He needed her to feel how hard he was, what she did to him. "Tease me, will you? You and that shower have starred in my dreams for days, I'll have you know. Dark, midnight dreams where I smudge you up so I can clean you off again."

"I want that," she whispered.

It was a good thing noises flitted around him to remind him they were in the middle of a busy barn full of working men and women. Bullet barreled into their space at that minute, barking and flopping around Cass, begging for love. Adam would have had her naked, screaming his name in minutes, she stirred him up that much.

"You promised me a ride," Cass said when he groaned into her. Gracie hung her head over the stall and neighed. She'd heard her favorite word now and she was one impatient lady.

The afternoon's light did not disappoint as they meandered their way up the rise above the main farm.

"She's itching to go fast," Cass said, atop Gracie, who pranced in place and stirred her head around, barely restraining herself.

"Let her go," Adam said and tipped his hat. And his ladies were off, racing across the field. Gracie's lean body was meant for running. Cass leaned over her and handled the horse like she'd been born riding, speaking to the beasts, hearing their language in her heart. He could tell by the way Gracie flew that she understood Cass, recognized her, was showing off for her. Sunlight spread its golden rays over the dried-out grasses and Cass and his Gracie danced through it all. He watched them as they neared the rise and circled back, and when they met him, he gave his horse the command and they all flew together back to the top of the hill, stopping when they reached the two old wisteria trees.

Adam helped Cass down from her horse, because he needed to touch her, and before her feet met the ground, he captured her joy with his mouth for a long, earth-shattering kiss.

"That was glorious."

I know. Is she talking about the ride or the kiss? "It's been years since I've ridden." She snuggled her body into his.

Adam gripped her with restraint, stalked away from her and tossed his hat onto the ground, his frustration all but shredding his jeans.

When she came up behind and wrapped her arms around him, he took a moment to calm his breathing. There was nothing to be done about being hard—his body jumped at her presence. He couldn't help it. He wanted to mate with her, mark her, make her his. Want he couldn't control, but he could control how he treated her, and even though it was sweet torture, he would go slow for her.

"I didn't mean to tease, not then." She stretched her body up so she whispered in his ear.

"All I have to do is look at you, think about you, and I'm wound up harder than a boulder."

She buried her face in his back and laughed. He loved her throaty laugh, her teasing, her not teasing— all of it. He'd strolled through life believing it full and bountiful before, but now it overflowed with waterfalls and he was in no rush to put a stopper in it. He relished the flood.

"Come, I want to show you something." Adam linked their fingers together and walked her up to the crest of the gently sloping field.

"Wow." Cass leaned her shoulder into his. Spread out before them was rolling pasture, as far as the eye's reach, almost. It met the water and the ocean sparkled and swayed into forever.

"It's where I'm going to build a home." A pile of rubble sat where the original house once resided. His great grandparents had built it, the first structure on

Brockman land. Next to it, a barn that would most likely crumble if someone sneezed on it. "Forgotten land, we used to call it when we were kids. Turner and Cruz and I would come up here and create imaginary worlds. We fought Vikings, seized castles, battled the fieriest dragons with swords traded from elves. I avoided it after they left." A few months ago, when the brothers had undertaken to split the land, he'd parked his Airstream here, staked his claim.

She walked the land with him until he pulled her down in a sunny spot not too far from the wisteria. No person had listened to him so closely, held his words carefully. He wondered if she heard the words in his heart that he was too afraid to say yet.

"Right here on the top of this hill, with the morning sunrise over the trees to the east, and a view of the sunset over the land and water every night. Knowing the land and animals and trees are all taken care of, seen to, loved." It was what he wanted, to belong, to be loved. He wanted to be loved by Cassandra Dorsey. He knew it as sure as he knew every inch of this land.

"I want to kiss you here." Adam lay down in the grass and pulled her over him. He was right. She was a fairy. They flitted around her in the field, her skin lustrous. "Under the sunlight, in a wild field. It's how I picture you, beauty surrounded by beauty. Can I kiss you here, Cassandra?"

And when she nodded, he swept them both away on the current that hummed between them in a chorus of lazy and intense kisses warmed by the sun, the heated ground and their passion. *I want you to make a home with me here.* He pressed the words into each kiss, each caress of his fingers to her soft warm skin. *Stay, here with me.*

At sunset, she sat between his legs with his arms encompassing her and they watched the sky turn orange and pink before leading their horses back in a slow walk as if neither one wanted to leave the forgotten land and all it signified now. Before duty and chores pulled them both back to reality.

Chapter Twenty

The next few days, Cassandra did not get to sit in the Brockman kitchen and indulge her pastry addiction. In her past life, she'd always favored the savory, the salty, tart and sometimes bitter flavors. A past life, foreign to her, so far away. She'd been a different person when Nathan had been alive and a different person since his death, and now another layer of her had sloughed off to reveal even more parts of herself, evolving each day in this gorgeous land. Like this incessant craving for all things sweet and doughy. Sweet *fried* dough was even better. And even though she could lament not having her daily, or rather multiple times daily, morning bun or pecan Danish, or cinnamon roll, it was all going to be worth it.

The family was preparing for their very first barn dinner celebration. They planned on offering them to the public come spring, but this one was for family, friends and locals who had become *family*. Cass had been invited. It was almost Sunday and she couldn't wait. Another thing that eased her disappointment at not being surrounded by baked goods every day was that she wasn't simply putting words to paper, but that her soul was back. It settled and sighed deep inside her. A return, a renewal.

She wrote, she snacked, she cooked a few meals, she napped and she wrote some more, only stepping foot in reality to chat with Annie or text with Adam or exchange a few hot kisses when he stopped by in the evenings. Lovely, slow, make-out kisses and nothing more. She didn't know if it was still for her benefit or not, but she couldn't wait for more with him, too. He'd shared something more important than a favorite spot with her when he'd taken her riding up to the forgotten land, as he'd called it. And she wanted him to know his dreams and desires were safe with her.

Is it odd that he doesn't have a house yet? It reminded her again how young he was, just starting out, the world his oyster. She envied him that, wanted to climb in his lap and share it all. Everything in her stirred with want. And what had been a lovely place for fantasy, her shower, was now one extreme source of frustration. He was everywhere, surrounding her, in her dreams in her waking hours. Unfortunately, with the duties of a farmer in late fall and the upcoming barn dinner, he was also desperately busy.

* * * *

Lily offered to pick her up and walk over with her. A few moments of nervousness had tripped through her brain when she'd been getting dressed. '*Barn dance chic,*' Lily had told her. Fashion wasn't what troubled her, but rather something elusive. Tonight, she and

Adam would share the evening with more than horses and dogs. His family and all his friends would be there. Would she fit in? His family had made no bones about accepting her, pulling her to their warmth and camaraderie. But this was so much more. It was the town Adam loved and took pride in, old friends he'd had since birth, his legacy.

Perhaps it was longing that tugged at her, for those things she would never have. Not that she'd trade her travels and moves for anything, but roots and life-long connections were truly a wonderful thing. *Making a family with someone out of love.* She'd tried it once and it had disappeared in a matter of seconds.

"I am so excited for this night. This family and this town deserve so much goodness." Lily's words shrugged her out of her musings.

"You sound almost angry." Cass squeezed Lily as they walked arm in arm under an umbrella big enough for the Grand Canyon.

"I prefer passionate, but yes. I won't bother you with the details tonight, but a black cloud hovered over this place when T.D. Brockman was alive. Especially for Katie and her sons, but also with anyone who crossed his path. Now, tonight a special crowd of people will light up the night and shatter all the last dregs of darkness he cast upon us."

"Sounds very Shakespearean."

"Oh, indeed."

Cass laughed at Lily's seriousness, her drama. No matter what her nerves got up to, someone around here was always putting her at ease, even if they didn't realize it. One more layer of safety and beauty to tuck into her new foundation of growth, of strength, of recovery.

Lily rested the umbrella outside the barn door, took Cass' hand and led her inside. "Wow! It looks beautiful," she said, her voice laced with awe.

Beautiful was an understatement. The barn was dressed up like she was going to her first party. Sparkly lights cast shimmers over the people gathered. Gorgeously set tables with platters of food and overflowing bouquets of flowers. Joy and excitement vibrated through the crowd. *Oh!* "Do they know everyone?" Bitterness slipped into Cass' words before she could camouflage it. Her flicker of comfort snuffed out.

Directly across the barn Adam stood smiling at someone, a young woman. Of course she was young and beautiful with perfect blonde hair flipping around her shoulders, like from a movie. They fit together. Young, golden, sun-kissed skin to Adam's reddish, tan hard muscles. *They* both wore barn chic like it was their natural grace while Cass knew she stood out with her designer clothes. Even jeans and a sweater could be snotty. She didn't want to be snotty or convey any sense of costume of hiding tonight. She wanted to be herself.

Lily scanned the barn and when she caught on, she slapped her hand over her mouth before the laughter notified everyone around them that they'd been staring. "That's Morgan. She's fifteen and probably giving an extremely long soliloquy about horses." Lily patted her back.

"Are you sure? Those look like lovesick eyes to me," Cass said.

"She's only lovesick for one thing—riding horses. Trust me." Lily faced her. "Plus, they're cousins. Wait till he notices you." Lily gazed over Cass' outfit.

"You're hot! More importantly, that man is connected to you like a magnet."

Cass relaxed a bit under Lily's confidence. And her new friend was right, the room shifted when Adam noticed her. Everything around them faded away as he made his way toward her, not even glancing back to the young, beautiful blonde. His face was set in a secret smile. He'd let his beard grow in a bit and it was a shade darker than his red hair. And those blue eyes, steady with intention, narrowed in on one thing, her.

"Evening, Cassandra." He took her hand and kissed it like an old-fashioned gentleman. Part playful, part authentic Adam, charming her with his confidence and wooing again. Every time it made her heart take flight. Like she was precious, lovable, like she deserved his goodness and his desire for her.

"And Lily," Lily chimed in.

"Looking beautiful as always, Liliana," Adam said without taking his eyes off Cass.

"Mmm-hmm," Lily said, knowingly, before she kissed Cass' cheek and left them there under the soft barn lights. There was a crowd of people, but her senses focused only on the two of them.

Adam wrapped one arm around her and danced them slowly in a tight circle.

"Is there music?" she asked. Her hand found the hair on his neck and she toyed with it. He watched her with that hidden hawk-like intensity.

"There should be. It's how I feel when I'm with you, holding you—like I'm hearing music for the first time ever. My body needs to move or my heart might jump out of my skin."

"I think I'm ready to dance with you tonight, Adam."

He nearly choked and it was only a small measure of relief that he felt as needy as she did.

"Let's go." He took her hand and started to drag her out of the barn.

"Adam," she hushed and glanced around. "We can't miss dinner."

"Oh, I'm pretty certain we can."

She tugged to get him to stop. "This is a special night for you."

He nodded and tried to angle her out again, but she dug in her heels and laughed.

"We have all night after this dinner to dance, and I may be a bit rusty but I'm a pretty good dancer." *Bet I'll be an awesome dancer with you.*

He pulled her tight and rested his forehead on hers. "You would tease a man in my condition. Have you any idea, woman?" He had a condition all right and it was pressed up against her, trying to lure her out into the wild night with him.

"Have a seat everyone and let's get this party started!" Cruz yelled. Thank goodness for interruptions or she might have lost her mind and let Adam and his condition lure her away from this monumental family event he would regret missing. She felt lucky to be by his side for it. Hopefully they'd both get lucky in a different way later.

She leaned up and whispered in his ear as he led her to their places next to each other at one of the long tables, "Besides, we'll need sustenance for all that dancing we're going to do later."

His tamped down growl made her laugh again. Once they sat, he took her hand in his and rested it on this thigh.

Cruz spoke again and everyone quieted around them, Hopefully they couldn't all hear the thudding of her heart. "Tonight is a celebration," the oldest brother began. "I think I speak for all of us when I say it's been a long damn time coming, all of us here together, peacefully for this new beginning. My family and I thank you for coming, for supporting us, for taking care of us all those years when we needed your help and didn't even realize we were getting it. Brockman Farms would not be around today if it weren't for all of you, for Graciella, for this community. Now we begin a new Chapter of friendship, love and abundance."

Everyone cheered and hollered. Cruz took his seat beside Miranda, music filtered around them and people began passing amazingness. Grilled legs of lamb. Soft and chewy rolls with salted rosemary butter, one of Miranda's new recipes that Cass took two of because she couldn't resist. The yeasty scent and warm rosemary were a perfume she craved. Wild greens with pomegranates and mashed potatoes.

All of it was incredible, the colors the aromas, like an Instagram drool-worthy setting. There was wine from a local winery that Cass had read about too, although she passed on the wine, wanting to be in complete sense of her body and mind and heart tonight. She was drooling. She was starving for all of it, save maybe the roasted carrots. As soon as the platter was passed to her, the spicy scent assaulted her in a way she had to choke back bile that rose instantly in her throat.

"Okay?" Adam asked when he took the platter from her.

"Guess when your sense of smell comes back after being gone for two years, it has a few glitches. Everything else smells amazing."

"Indeed." He smirked at her. "I think you were right about staying and gaining energy. I'm starving. And I haven't eaten in a long, long time, Cassandra."

Goodness, she was right back to melting into a lusty pile of erotic Adam dreams.

Chapter Twenty-One

"What a wonderful thing you've made here," Cassandra said. She sat next to Katie and Miranda at the end of one of the long tables, the remains of dinner and splendor, family and party strewn across the tables. The barn was still abuzz with talking and laughing and people dancing to the music. A few had straggled home, but joy still permeated the evening.

Adam stood not too far away, at the bar he and his brothers had built specifically for these dinners. He'd been in conversation with them, but he followed Cassandra with his gaze and his ears perked up whenever her voice reached him. His entire body was tuned into her voice.

"It was lovely." Katie Brockman clasped her hand. "I was just telling Miranda how much joy and love she's brought to this place."

So have you, he wanted to whisper to Cassandra, trail his fingers down her graceful back, twine their hands together, flirt with the delicate skin on her wrist. Holding back his words of love for her and what she meant to him already in such a short time was more difficult than taking the physical slowly. Could she not see his emotions scored in ink across his skin?

"I'd call tonight a success," Cruz said, dragging his attention back. "What about you two?"

"Mmm." Adam nodded.

"T.D. would have hated it," Cruz added.

"To T.D. hating every second of our love and success." Turner's voice was hard and defiant. He clinked his bottle against theirs. Adam wanted to get to Cass.

"To be honest," Turner continued, "I never imagined this day."

Cruz nodded. "It was difficult, wasn't it? Nearly impossible at times to hope that he'd ever be gone and we could finally breathe free."

Adam's face tightened. *He'd* imagined it. He'd stayed through all of it. Even after high school when his mother had said he could go anywhere for college, he hadn't left. The degree in Agriculture and Farm Management from the community college was all he needed, wanted. Leaving the land, leaving his belief in the farm hadn't been an option for him, no matter how mean and nasty T.D. had been. Adam had known it would all survive. Therefore, he would survive, only suspended in time before they could thrive again. He'd endured it all. And he'd do it again in a heartbeat.

He wondered if his brothers knew the price he'd paid in staying and how every single second of that price was worth it. It wasn't that he was better than them. Each one had had their own path to follow. But knowing in his soul where he was meant to be and that it was on Brockman land only made this moment that much sweeter.

"I want to ask your permission to send my essays about you all to my old editor at the paper." Cass' words drew his gaze again. Such hope shone on her pretty face, skin glowing in the low lights.

Katie and Miranda gushed over the idea. This was their dream, really. He and his brothers had wanted to be free of T.D., to be free to love this place. But Miranda, Katie, Lily, with her grand new construction of the café, were responsible for fertilizing and growing a whole new Chapter for the family. His heart split open again for Cass in that moment, that she understood how much this meant to them, that she wanted to help them, to celebrate them and their endeavors.

"He's got it bad."

"Bet he doesn't have a clue what he's doing."

"All right, yahoos, I hear you," Adam faced his brothers with a grin.

"Did you tell her yet?" Cruz, usually teasing him, was serious now. He knew. Both his brothers did. Maybe it was carved into his expression.

"Trying not to scare her away," Adam admitted. "She's lived quite a life already." He wanted to confide in them about her marriage, about his uncertainty, that he wasn't enough for her. *Will I ever be enough for someone?*

"Haven't we all." Javier, more father than T.D. had ever been, joined them. Adam doubted Javier knew that he'd saved Adam's life too when he'd swept Katie off her feet all those years ago and taken Adam with them when they'd left Brockman House. One of the worst and best days of his life. One last sip of beer chased down his emotions at the memories.

"It's a good thing we get more than one chance in life." His wisdom anointed them all. "Shouldn't waste those chances wondering. A little risk is good for the heart."

"You're lucky you had him," Turner said to Javier's retreating back. Katie met him halfway and they took to the dance floor.

"Yeah," Adam said. *Lucky because you two left. Left the land behind, our legacy, me.* He needed fresh air suddenly. It wasn't a thought he had often. *No sense dwelling on the past.* He was the quick-witted, funny brother. He made do, got along with everyone, put his heart into his work, his dreams.

Having Javier in his life did make him lucky, no doubt about that. But the truth was so much deeper. He'd hated it when his brothers had left. Hated *them* for a few moments when despair snuck up and tried to drag him down. Deep inside, there was a part of him that had never fully healed, even though they'd returned. Until now, until Cassandra had stepped in and mended the small dark hole in his heart.

Chapter Twenty-Two

"Well, if it isn't the prettiest lady I've ever seen." Adam's voice, deep and resonant, caressed her. He leaned against the open barn door, cast like a warrior in the moonlight. The moon was now a sharp orb in the midnight sky after the rain and clouds had passed.

It was as if the deepest breath she'd ever taken surged through her, giving her belief, freeing her, beckoning a new world of enchanted delights and seduction. It was huge and all-encompassing. It scared and thrilled her. A tingling started in her feet and wound itself up her limbs, setting each molecule alight. The fresh damp landscape and all its cooling scents erupted around her, bare tree limbs glassy with leftover raindrops, soil, hints of the firewood crisp in the clean night, and Adam's scent striking through them all. *Adam, Adam, Adam*, her heart murmured. *I recognize you.*

"You've been seeing me all night." Cass walked right into his arms. It was so easy and wonderful to find her place with him.

He kissed her, right there under the mysterious sky, like he couldn't breathe if his body didn't connect with hers immediately. She'd gladly be his breath. Something buzzed about him. Perhaps it was the full moon and silvery fantastical light, the possibility, or perhaps it was his desire. He cradled her face and held her to him while his lips sculpted against hers, learning, awakening, being reborn.

Starlight exploded through her skin, speaking languages of love and need and cherishing. With his arms wrapped around her, he moved their bodies in a slow mimic of the twirl he'd done earlier, dancing them to their own musical score.

"Every time I'm struck again, like it's the first time all over. My heart wakes up alive and wonderful from beneath my ribs to reach yours." There was a fervor to his words, his hands, an undoing, an unraveling about his tightly held, kind control. A hint of all the dark things he wanted to do to her. The connection, that secret charge revved inside her blood making her want everything he had to give.

Introduce me to your darkness. Cass linked her hands around his neck, sneaking her fingers under the collar of his shirt to discover his warm skin. Her soft body wanted closer, to feel all the hard ridges of him. "Our hearts are beating together," she whispered against his lips. How difficult it was not to kiss him every second, but how wonderful it was at the same time to speak like this, connected under their own fairy lights of desire and magic. It swirled around them. If this was what she meant by being fully engaged of senses, of mind, of body, of heart, then she would bare it all for him. No more hiding, no more careful waiting. Her heart felt safe with his and alive too, frantically alive.

"Cassandra." He took her lips again, greedy, devouring as he came to her, the starving man he'd claimed to be now feasting on her. "You bewitch me." He nipped at her ear. "You claim me." He dragged his lips down her neck. "I'm yours. I've never been anyone's, but now I'm yours." With his lips still learning hers, he gently set her down. "Let me walk you home." *Be mine,* beat from his heart to hers. *Let me have you.*

"Yes." She nodded.

His body braced. And with a gentle caress he brushed her hair back and searched her eyes. *I wonder if mine are glowing like his, enchanted by the sorcery around them and in them.*

"Please," she answered his unspoken question. "I'm sure." His smile widened even as his eyes darkened further. *With desire? With promise?* Whatever thread he'd been holding on to snapped. And how spectacular it was. He pulled her to him and practically bent her over with the force of his kiss. Her lips felt bruised, gloriously as she met his need. With his unleashing, he'd set her desires free as well.

They didn't so much walk back to her cottage as stumble for all the kissing and sighing and groping. She was surprised they made it back at all. How lovely it would be to make love with him under the moonlight someday, on that field he'd shown her, for all the stars to witness.

"You're all wet," he said it as if it were a challenge or an accusation, her very own teasing and seduction. How could he know how wet she was for him? "Your hair, so pretty covered with raindrops, and here..." He drew a finger down her neck tracing droplets. She immediately arched to him, her senses on overload. A light rain had begun to fall, hovering over them in nature's beauty. A chill had blown in with the rain. The air around them swirled with a hint of cold and hibernation. *Nearly winter now.*

"Come," Cass whispered and walked him into her warm lair. Even before the door closed, they had each other's tops off. And she gasped at his body while her hands ached to explore. So deliciously huge and hard, all his muscles earned from a lifetime of labor, his body was its own dance to behold. He shook his hair and the droplets seared her skin. She ached and didn't know whether to touch herself or touch him. But her hands found their way to his chest.

"Cassandra," he hissed out in reverence. "Your fingers are frozen."

"I don't feel the cold. Only your heat," she said as she roamed his chest greedily, first with light brushes of her lips, then her hands.

"It's both of us. It's madness. Sweet, beautiful madness. Don't want to be sane again," he said as he claimed her body and tugged it flush against his. He leaned down to place a kiss on her chest so close to her aching breasts which were heavy and needy for him.

Please kiss me everywhere. But words deserted as he took her mouth again. He lifted her and she laughed at the surprise and pleasure of his big hands cradling her ass. Ever since the night on her couch when he'd brought her to orgasm with that same caress, she'd craved it.

"It's been building since we first sparred in the sunlight, and now a full moon and all this want, all your teasing texts about showers. Now I have you all wet, do you want to know what I want? To warm you up in the water. To have you naked in that shower. I can't stop thinking about it, craving it." They were upstairs before she knew it, more of the magic luring them along. Then naked they stood before each other. "Did you hear me, Cassandra? I crave you."

All she could do was nod. Had anyone ever craved her before? What was before? Nothing from then mattered. Not time or age or past loves. All that mattered and gave her life was Adam as he took her hand and led her under the waterfall. And it was nothing like what she imagined. So much bigger and more crowded. Oh, how she loved his naked body taking up space in that glorious shower, in her heart. A heart that she'd thought might stay numb forever now beat joyously for another.

Chapter Twenty-Three

"Finally," Adam groaned when his hands met her flesh. The hot cascading water surrounded them. It opened his senses, tried to increase his desire. But his desire for her was a living breathing galaxy all on its own. Before he had a chance to walk her to the wall and attach their bodies, she massaged her hands up his chest and linked them again behind his head, pulling him down as she rose to meet him, dragging her body against his. His hard cock against her pelvis, her breasts soft and luscious against his muscles. Her glorious body all right here for his pleasure, his salvation.

"You've been starring in my shower fantasies." Cass closed her eyes and tilted her head to catch the stream of water on her face. Her hands unlinked and before his gaze she roamed them over her own body, gripping her breasts, steering lower. "At night when I can't sleep, in the morning when I step in here. You're all I can think about. You cloud my brain."

"Is this what you do when you want me and you're all alone?" He gripped her hips and rubbed the pads of his thumbs into her skin at those beautiful spots where curves dived in, silky skin over carved bone. His eyes followed the path of his thumbs. Her moans pounded through his ears, water heightening every sensation.

"Jesus, woman. I need to taste you." He pivoted her against the wall then, all patience gone, and knelt in front of her, taking in every expanse of her skin available to him. He had so much to explore. "I want to know all of you. And, Cassandra..." His gaze met the seduction in her own eyes. "I'm a greedy, greedy man," he said before he placed his mouth right there, over his own personal dessert he'd been dreaming about all through dinner.

"Yes!" Her acceptance, her pleasure came to him via her words and her body, arching her core into his mouth. He feasted, snaking out his tongue and licking up her sensitive swollen skin, over and over again. Her body trembled under his touch. Water cascaded over them. He took her bud into his mouth and sucked on it while kneading his thumbs lower and lower until he found his treasure. He pushed two fingers into her pussy that was drenched for him.

"Yes, yes, yes," she chanted. Unabashedly, she ran her fingers through his hair and held his head where she wanted it until she crashed over the edge and came apart in a million pieces for him.

Fucking beautiful goddess. All mine. And this is only the beginning. He steadied them both with his arms around her as he rose, and while she rested her head on his shoulder, he soaped up the sponge and sudsed her gorgeous dewy skin. Cleaning and caressing and soothing every delicious inch of her.

When he turned off the water, she clung to him. "I don't think I can walk." She kissed and nipped at his skin, suckling drops of water into her mouth. "Better than any fantasy. Wow."

He lifted her out of the shower and dried them off before he carried her spent and flushed body to the bed.

She clung to his neck when he made to leave. "Stay with me tonight, Adam. Make love to me again."

His blood, already an inferno, surged at those words along with his cock. *Down boy*, he commanded. *Hey, we left slow behind us in the rain*, his cock demanded.

Cass' eyes were heavy and happy. A hint of dark circles lingered under her eyes, but at least she was exhausted now for good reasons. And he had no qualms about feeling smug.

"Be right back." He kissed her. The chill shocked him as soon as he snuck naked down the stairs to find his jacket. Thank fuck he'd gone the hopeful route and added condoms to his pockets.

"Your sexy farmer returns."

But that joke was on him tonight. Cassandra was sound asleep, already lost in dreamland when he returned. He huffed out a laugh. "Guess being hard is in my permanent future around you, gorgeous." Adam snuggled in behind her, wrapped his arm around her soft sleeping form and let himself dream of a life of discovering all the ways he could make Cass happy.

* * * *

Cass woke with a start from the best dream ever, hot and bothered and...needing to use the bathroom. A house might as well have been sitting on her bladder. When she was finished, the light from the bathroom bathed her bed in a warm glow. *Oh.* She touched her chest. *Not a dream at all.* Her heart did its flippity-flops again. Naked and sexy Adam asleep in her bed. Her entire body flushed with the memory of that shower.

"Hey, gorgeous." His gruff voice startled her perusal of his body lying on his side facing her. *So not asleep, nope.* Not one single part of him was down for the count. Especially not the part she wanted first-hand knowledge of. The shower hadn't given her enough time. He'd done so many wonderful things to her and she'd passed out on him. *Guess that's what a fantastic shower orgasm does.*

"You stayed." She knelt into the bed and placed her hand on his chest. He tugged her down next to him and draped his leg over hers, cinching her to him where she could feel how awake and greedy he was, pulsing against her. She'd wanted to return the attention after their shower, but sleep had dragged her down in seconds.

Adam nuzzled into her neck and started that seduction-by-lips he was so amazing at, but she didn't need to be seduced now. She was already on cloud nine. Now it was her turn to give pleasure. Cass wiggled out of his grip and moved lower, using her fingertips to flirt with his skin. "I've been dreaming of how you'd taste too, sexy farmer," she said right before she took hold of his rock-hard length and took him into her mouth.

He gripped the sheets in restraint, but his body surged up. "Fuck, Cass," he hissed. The man was epically gifted in restraint, in control, in waiting for her, but *she* wanted him unleashed and loved what she could do to him to make him lose control around her. She trusted him and that added to the aphrodisiac of Adam Brockman. Swirling her tongue, she teased and sucked, using her hands to stroke his skin while his body surged and rippled beneath her. So much of his skin she wanted to kiss and tantalize. It gave her pleasure to give to him, watching his massive body jerk and swear under her, watching her kind, patient, charming man harden and lose control. And the way he swore her name like a benediction, like a promise of torture and pleasure in return...

Suddenly she was gripped in his arms. He dragged her up his body, forcing all her tingling parts, her hard, aching nipples, her belly, her thighs to drag against his skin and she stretched like a jungle cat, wanton, free and hungry. He was wild now too. He sucked her nipples one after the other, nearly biting, then lifted her higher so he could kiss and lick at her belly. A fire shimmered inside her, her core burning and calling to him. And before she could brace herself on the headboard, he'd lifted her even higher and kissed the neediest place of her where all the blood rushed and panted and begged. He sucked and nipped at her core like a desperate animal, his hands gripping her hips in fierce possession while he took what he wanted, what she freely gave.

"I need you, Cass." He tossed her onto the bed next to him, reached over and grabbed a condom. "Let me have you?"

"I need you too." Cass took the condom from his shaking hands and rolled it on him.

Adam gripped her hands above her head and surged in. "Adam," she breathed. Her body chased and writhed toward his.

"Gorgeous woman." He didn't kiss her, but his gaze promised *everything*. The word whispered around her, from his heart to hers. His eyes, dark and wild, free and happy, full of desire and longing, the way he spoke with them, was her heart's complete undoing. He pulled out in slow torture and thrust back in, picking up the pace in a frenzy.

"Let me touch you." She arched into him.

He shook his head and drove in, each stroke taking her higher. Her blood, her core, burned to be set free. "Next time. Now is for me. I want to watch you, watch your body move beneath mine, cat-like and needy. Watch those eyes of yours heat and darken with want for me. Do you know how much I ache for you? Even when I'm inside you, even when you claim me like this, I want."

He was too big, his heart, his desire, bigger than she could handle, as he ground his body close to hers, bringing her higher, bringing them both higher, stroking her body with the flame burning from his eyes, branding her. He body shook as she squeezed him inside her. Cass soared with power when he lost control. Letting go of her arms to wrap them together in a wild tornado of energy, he rocketed them both into space.

Cass wanted to snuggle and kiss and speak of amazing sensations, of *feeling* again, of all these new emotions fluttering inside her, but as soon as Adam left the bed, her familiar coma of sleep dragged her under. And, sated, wrapped in knowledge and power, she dreamed of wild things, of spells of love twining around her and Adam in a field of flowers with the ocean at their feet, while the words *I love you* moved across the clouds and into her heart.

Chapter Twenty-Four

The irony of the days getting shorter even while Adam's workdays grew longer in this end-of-season time blared like a bad commercial at the front of his brain. Gathering, harvesting, closing and hibernating some things until spring. He'd just as soon skip over winter. It was time for a good long nap, the only thing Adam appreciated in winter, and now he couldn't wait to do it with his long-legged beauty.

Napping had taken on a whole new meaning for him and he aimed to take advantage of all that under-the-covers time. He chuckled at how much she liked her sleep, how he'd returned to bed last night and found her far away in dreamland again. The woman slept like a champion. She'd also teased and tortured his body into sweet oblivion last night. He was hard again with the memories of her sweet, sweet warmth. Maybe he could convince her to stay in bed until March.

Stay forever. The words beat through his mind. His heart, his love. He loved her as sure as the waves crashed into the shore and circled back. Love was amazing, fluid heat and life, power and want and desire to give, all wrapped into the most beautiful person he'd ever encountered because she was his and he was hers. Their hearts belonged together. It steadied him and took him soaring at the same time. As certain as he'd ever been of anything. He wanted to tell her that he loved her, that he wanted to make a life with her, build a house for her. She gave him *everything*. An unrepayable gift, but he'd gladly spend every day trying.

Where is she? He'd been thinking of her all day. Those lips, her warm body clamping around his, soft skin and eyes like a sorceress. *Does she think about me the way I think about her? Should I tell her she makes little mew sounds in her dreams? What does she dream about? Can she feel my heart beating for hers even in her dreams?*

But wondering where she was and daydreaming about her slowly turned to alertness. She and Gracie hadn't returned from their ride. He'd wanted to go with her, but he'd had back-to-back appointments concerning horses, boarding more and lessons for a friend in town. It was later than he realized, and the rains had returned. *Damn rain.* A farmer rarely cursed the rain, but there were times when it was a menace. Late November coupled with a sharp drop in temperature was not a welcome time for rainstorms on a farm.

A hint of worry started behind his eyes. She should have been back by now. Adam walked by the stalls, double-checking. Gracie's was still empty. Damn, it would be dark soon, too. Without hesitation, he saddled up Orion, intending to search for her. Cass was a good rider, but no one enjoyed riding in this weather.

Had something happened? The rain turned to a downpour right as Bullet raced toward him, growling and barking up a frenzy around Adam, demanding his attention. The dog was soaked to the bone. His barks were insistent and loud, not cute puppy yips and playful shenanigans. His mutt was all business, and the hackles on the back of Adam's neck stood up and took notice.

"What's up, boy?"

Bullet thundered out of the barn. Adam grabbed a flashlight, mounted his horse and followed.

"What in the ever-loving hell has gotten into you?" Adam yelled as Bullet raced down the path to the beach. Frozen slashes of rain assaulted him. It was a dangerous storm to be caught in, worse as the black clouds were snuffing out the last stretch of daylight, and his pulse kicked up in fear.

Gracie's angry neighs, a banshee through the rain, attacked his ears. She was huffing and shaking her mane.

Jesus Christ! Terror snuffed out his heartbeat. Cass lay on the beach next to Gracie, who was sending out her own warning alarm matching Bullet's for intensity as the two animals hovered around his woman.

"Cassandra," he yelled over the rain and wind. She startled and squinted open her eyes and his life passed before him.

"I...what happened? I hurt..." She pulled herself to a sitting position and touched her head. *Thank fuck she's moving.*

"You were riding. You fell or fainted, I don't know. Bullet found you, led me here." She slumped against him and he wrapped his arm around her. "I've got you now." He cradled her and dialed Cruz's number under the relentless rain.

"Cruz, I need help, down at the beach. Cass is hurt. Call an ambulance. I need you to come get the horses. I'm carrying her up."

She gripped his arm. "Something's wrong. I..." Cass looked down her body. "I don't feel right."

"Let's get you to the hospital, darlin'." He tried to use gentle words to keep the fear at bay for both of them. "I'm going to pick you up now. I'll try not to hurt you." It took all his power not to lose it as he lifted her shivering body into his arms. Blood ran bright red from a gash on her forehead as it mixed with the rainwater and sluiced off her cheek.

"The horses," she cried into his chest, her arms limp on her body.

"Hush. Cruz will get them."

"I don't know what happened. I felt weird like I was going to be sick. I tried to get off Gracie... I blacked out, I think. It's so cold. I'm so, so cold."

Adam held on tight as he climbed, hoping he wasn't hurting her in the process but wanting to get her up the slippery cliff path as quickly as possible.

Setting her down on the stretcher to let the paramedics take care of her was more difficult than carrying her up the muddy slope from the beach in the downpour. He wanted to keep her locked in his arms where he could warm her, heal her, protect her. He buckled in next to her in the ambulance, held her hand and tried to help answer the questions they fired at her.

Did she know her name? Who was Adam in relation to her? How had he found her? Had she eaten today? Did she have a history of fainting? Was she allergic to anything? Did she have any prior medical conditions?

Fay, the woman's nametag said. She asked her questions calmly, but seriously while her hands gently assessed Cass. Temperature was normal, blood pressure a little low, gauze to her wound. Fay took Adam's hand and placed it on the gauze to hold it in place while she wrote and checked off boxes on her clipboard. The ride blurred by while his heart attempted to catch up to what the fuck had happened.

Javier, his mother and Miranda met them at the emergency room. They tried to guide him away as the paramedics handed her stretcher off to the nurses and doctors. "Sir, I need you to stay out here," Fay said, blocking Cass from his view as they wheeled her away.

"I'm not leaving her."

"Adam," his mother said. "You can't go with her. Come here."

He shrugged his arm out of her grip. "I'm not leaving her!"

Javier put his hands on his chest and shoved Adam out through the automatic doors. It was enough of a shock to have Adam coming back to himself. "Fuck!" He smacked his hands against the wet brick, swearing into the storm.

"Get that out of your system before you go back inside. I know you're worried. They'll take good care of her. You've known these doctors all your life. When you've calmed down, I brought you clothes to change into. You're soaked through."

Worried was too calm a word. His emotions raged as the storm did, furious and out of control. "I can't lose her. I finally found her. She found me," he bellowed.

Javier gripped his shoulder. "Listen to me, son, and you are my son. Maybe not by blood, but by bonds far stronger. In here" — Javier pounded on his chest —

"you're in love with her. And we're all here for you. As scared as you are right now, you need to pull yourself together so you can be there for *her*."

Adam slumped against him. The wind might as well have been knocked out of him for the force of those words and the breath they stole. He was too choked up to respond. He'd longed to be someone's son, worthy of that kind of love. Javier gripped him in a tight hug.

"Let's go in, son. Let's go see if they know anything."

Chapter Twenty-Five

Cass dragged herself from her nap when he arrived carrying a bag of almond croissants, her absolute favorite thing on Miranda's menu, all covered in powdered sugar and thin almonds. She could practically taste the contrast of all that soft sugar on the warm pastry dough. But instead of making her hungry, the smell lodged harsh and dry in her throat. Even her nap felt icky, weighted. Overnight her entire life had morphed. Again.

Would she ever right her tilted world? The tears came unbidden again. *Fucking tears*. It didn't even help to know why she'd been a leaky faucet lately, why the extreme exhaustion. The fainting and strange food cravings, even her renewed sense of smell couldn't be attributed to healing, or falling in love with a dream man. She rubbed her stomach, softly pressing on her body. *Will I love you? Will you love me?* Love had so many more meanings than she'd ever realized, each one unique and a bundle of layers. No easy definition to it.

Bullet snuggled on her feet, watching her. He hadn't left her side all morning. She suspected he'd slept with them last night too.

Last night. Christ!

Adam had driven her home from the hospital, had taken such good care of her, slept with her in case she needed him. And she hadn't told him the truth, not all of it. The shock mixed with her fatigue had stolen her words, and they'd drained away with the rivulets of rain drenching the truck's window. How could she say what she could barely comprehend? *Fainting spell* was all she'd told him. One big doozy of a fainting spell.

She wanted to tell him the rest, here now, away from all the doctors and assessing eyes but how did one pull the rock from the cliff that would have all the others tumbling down around, crushing them in the landslide?

"Hey, pretty darlin'." There was more concern than tease in his voice. But she wanted to grasp on to that *darlin'* because as much silly crap as she'd given him over it, she loved it and wanted it for herself for always. She wanted him to promise to call her darlin' again after she'd explained. Sadly, it was most likely the last endearment she'd hear from him.

"Everybody sends hugs. They're all concerned about you. Miranda made get-well treats." He sat down in front of her on the coffee table, setting the bag of croissants beside him. "Scared the daylights out of me," he whispered. His hand shook in hers and she gripped it tightly once before she pulled herself up to sitting and dragged the throw blanker around her shoulders.

This man. His heart. He loved her as surely as she loved him. Even without the words, she could sense it. And it was never going to be hers to carry, to nurture. He deserved a true, unblemished love full of devotion, someone to give unconditionally, the way he gave.

"Feeling better?"

Cass rubbed her eyes. "Adam." Her gaze found his, and all boyish charm had gone. A worried, serious man sat before her, his heart exposed, waiting.

"It's worse, isn't it? Not just fainting spells."

"I'm pregnant," she blurted out. "Almost fourteen weeks."

An entire story played out over his face. Sentences of confusion, a body braced in tension, great and painful understanding, until he shadowed his emotions from her vision. Even Bullet tensed with the change in the air, his whine a question.

Adam stood and looked around as if he didn't know where he was.

"I'm sorry. I didn't know," she said. "Until last night."

He swallowed, made to say something, then, running his hands through all that thick red hair she loved, he paced to the window and braced his hands overhead, gripping the trim for dear life. Bullet inched closer up her lap and nudged his head under her hand, whimpering out his worry.

"But your husband was…is dead." He faced her, this time an open book of pain, or betrayal. It was worse than if he'd shown anger.

"He did die. I told you the truth." *Just not all of it.* "And I wished I had as well. For months I was a broken shell of myself. I told you…I explained some. What I didn't tell you was about six months ago how desperate

I was to *feel* again, anything other than sorrow or emptiness, to not be lonely, to have someone hold me. I was so damned lonely. Sick and tired of it." The words flowed with her tears, now unleashed. "I was stupid. I drank too much. Went on stupid dates. I wanted to... If I could meet someone, obliterate all the memories from my head and my heart, experience anything again for someone living... Well. The details aren't wonderful. I had a one-night stand. We used condoms. It was not great. He was gone in the morning." Cass gazed out of the window, shuddered. She remembered waking up the next morning, all by herself again. "Turns out I was still lonely. Maybe lonelier than before. Apparently the condoms didn't work either."

She struggled to take a breath. What a way to get pregnant, to *find out* she was pregnant, to tell Adam. Shame tried to slither under the edges of her mind, shake its finger at her, but she shoved it aside. What was done was done. Besides, there was no shame in a woman having casual sex with a man. But now she had to move forward, had to get her life together, and not merely on a whim but because a tiny human being needed her.

How still the air stretched between them. His silence propelled her on. "I didn't have a clue because I've hardly had a period at all since Nathan died. When he...when he was killed, I stopped eating regularly for a long time. Food might as well have been cardboard." And oh, how bitter it sat on her tongue now. "I lost a lot of weight and my cycle stopped, adapted, so I didn't...wasn't even... I hadn't made any connections these past few weeks with the way my body was acting."

The quiet drummed its fingers on her gut. He stood there, all his hard, beautiful planes, braced. Was he listening? Did he hear her?

"So you're with some...guy...then he casts you aside..." His voice was hoarse, words stripped bare and angry.

"Adam." She choked back the hurt. "Don't." Love was always so fucking painful. Crushing, really. "You don't get to make me feel bad for choices I made before I met you."

"No, Cass," he said harshly. Then softer, "I didn't mean it to come out like that. It's not what I intended. I thought we..."

We aren't anything anymore. Her own heart broke at the knowledge. "I didn't mean to hurt you, Adam, I..." *Love you. But I can't put that on you now.* "I think you should go. I have a lot to think about. I'm shocked and afraid for myself, for what this all means." She couldn't be around him, because she wanted his love and compassion. She wanted his arms to comfort her. Unfortunately, even if he could get over his disappointment in her, whatever path they'd started down wasn't meant to be. And that was one more wound she'd have to carry when she left. Because she had to. It was time to go home. *San Francisco. Is that really my home? It's so distant now.* A place she'd merely passed through to get here, to get to Adam, but it turned out neither Adam nor this beautiful place were meant for her, after all.

He took a step toward her, but she put her hand up. "Please, I need you to go."

"Cass," he pleaded in a deep, desperate voice, but she kept her head down. *Please go before I beg you to stay, beg you to still love me, beg you to want to be with me like this.* Moments stretched out between them in a thin thread before he finally cut it and walked out. Bullet jumped off the couch and barked at him. Then he slathered Cass' face with kisses.

"Go, boy," she commanded and pointed to the door. "Go find your human."

And when he followed her command, she didn't know whether to be happy he would be there to comfort Adam or brokenhearted as he ran away from her.

Chapter Twenty-Six

Loathe, abhor, despise. Despise was a good word to describe how Adam felt about winter. Too much time spent indoors catching up on paperwork, fixing equipment, planning for spring. Too much time alone. Too fucking cold. This one leeched at him appropriately bitter and stark.

Lonely. She'd spoken of loneliness like it was a living breathing thing, a physical ache, and he understood now. Even some of the horses wore blankets to keep them warm. It was the coldest winter they'd had on record. Brockman Farms was a frozen, barren landscape. Work he loved, like caring for the horses, did nothing but freeze his fingers, including the ones around his heart. Every damned thing was frozen.

Three weeks she'd been gone. It might have been three decades, millennia. How did one measure the time between when one's heart was ripped out of one's body to now? His laugh was hollow. What a stupid question. There was no fucking way to measure something so invisible yet painful. He'd never imagined after their last conversation that she would just leave. That it was the end.

It was a battle, what he despised more now, how outdoor things came close to a screeching halt on the farm, even the tractors packed away and silent, or the constant beating of his heart reminding him that he was alive. And that she was gone.

"Fucking freezing out today." Turner stood outside Gracie's stall as Adam brushed her coat and checked for any chaffing before he returned the blanket over her body.

"No kidding, jackass."

"Ahh, he speaks. He's still alive," Turner called to the office. "Pissed, but alive."

"I'm not pissed." *Ha!* Even Gracie could feel his anger. She side-stepped away from him then shoved his chest with her head. *Get your shit together!* she demanded. He tried to let the ache seep out of him. The animals could always tell when a person was on edge. He'd schooled many a student on the same thing. This was no place for him to be right now while he walked the knife edge of pain, of anger.

"Are you ever going to talk about it?" Turner asked. Cruz walked up and handed them coffees. They all knew what had happened. Cass had told the ladies the last morning before she'd left. When she'd told them goodbye. She hadn't bothered to say goodbye to him. *Probably because you behaved like both sides of a horse's ass.*

What the hell had even happened? He'd met her. Fallen in love. She'd broken his heart and left. *Wrong. You're the jackass. You shoved her away with your uncalled-for fucking ill-timed judgment. No wonder she was worried about the age difference. Acting like you're still fifteen with a chip on your shoulder.*

It grated at his nerves to think of how he'd behaved. He'd wanted to gather her in his arms and soothe away the dread in her expression, the bruise on her cheek, the hollow circles under her eyes. To tell her it would all be okay, but he'd been stuck, lodged under the frozen pond in shock with her news. Instead of taking care, he'd made it all about himself.

"She left. There's nothing to talk about." Coffee sluiced bitter on his tongue. It did nothing to warm him. All it did was stir up memories, churning them with acid in his stomach.

"You're in love with her, yet you're stomping around here like a bull, not going after her. Seems to me there's a lot to talk about," Cruz said.

He couldn't face them right now. His brothers were happy, in love, clueless. "People leave. It happens. Everyone has their own stuff to deal with. I get it." He tried to brush them off. "Got work to do." He needed them to go. He *got* nothing. He understood nothing. Not when *they'd* left, and fuck, not when they'd stayed away. The world threatened to crash down around him, and he couldn't deal with it.

"Her *stuff* was finding out she's pregnant and single, not to mention she's already lost a husband. Stop moping around and be there for her."

Adam wanted to knock Cruz flat for nailing it. It cut him to realize his heartbreak was nothing compared to what she must be going through, how scared she must be. Jesus, if he punched anyone, it should be himself.

"This isn't like you. You take care of people. You lead the way, you go after what you want, always have.

Boost everyone up. You don't let things get you down," Turner said.

"What the hell do you know about how I handle things?" he yelled. "Either of you?" He sliced them a glare. "You both disappear for more than a decade and suddenly you think you know anything about me, what kind of man I am." He shoved through them out of the stall and into the bleak gray day.

One more thing he hated about the winter, aside from the cold so harsh it burned, was the silence. Now it weighed like stones on his back, heavy, jagged, guilt. His breath came harsh, clouding the air before him in angry puffs.

"You're right." Turner stood next to him. Adam felt Cruz on his other side. Christ, he didn't want to fight with his brothers. Their presence in the face of his anger deflated his coiled emotions.

"I remember the first time it snowed for you, Adam, when we were kids. Or at least the first time I was old enough to make the memory. You were two or three. We'd had such dry winters. Mere sketches, Mom used to call them. Then that year, it was around this time, early December and the biggest, puffiest flakes drifted down, got heavier and faster. The ground turned white in the blink of an eye. I think we got over a foot during that storm.

"Sono, you called it from the porch window. And when we got all bundled up to go play in it, your laughter echoed over the land. Like music. Joyful, pure. For a little while, it shattered the heavy dark place that was so much of our lives. *Free and happy*, I remember thinking. How free and happy you made us all. Every time it snowed, a white blanket speckled over the land, hushed and brilliant, and you made us delight in it. You did that, *do* that for all of us every day."

"I'm sorry I stayed away for so long, that I left you behind. It was a shitty thing to do, I know it now," Turner chimed in.

"Same. I never realized it affected you like this," Cruz said.

"You are my big brothers, my family." Adam carved the words out of his throat, thick with emotion. Tears burned his eyes before they nearly froze on his cheeks. "You meant, *mean* everything to me. At fifteen you were my world. How the fuck did you think I would feel?" He scanned the dusty frozen landscape. "I know that you aren't responsible for my happiness. And shit, this place was a disaster for both of you, but I was a kid. I fucking missed the hell out of both of you." Exhaustion rolled over him. "The farm was my world. Then she came in and busted that world up into a million pieces. I screwed up and I don't know how to fix it. If it even can be fixed. She took all the magic and warmth with her."

"I don't think you get it, brother. You are what makes this world brilliant. When I was gone from here, all those years, thinking of you and Turner and all the fun we had all the trouble we got up to, those are the memories that kept me going, that brought me back here. You are responsible for that link. You're a good man, the best I know. I think you should go get her. Tell her how you really feel, lay it all out there."

"I was there when she said goodbye," Turner said. "She was miserable and lost. She looked like she didn't want to leave."

Fuck!

"How can I simply go get her?"

"I'm pretty sure we have these things called cars or airplanes—"

Adam punched Turner's shoulder. "She's having someone else's baby, idiot. Things are complicated."

"You're the idiot." Turner gave him a friendly shove back. "Do you love her?"

Adam nodded.

"Does she love you?"

He closed his eyes and wrapped himself in her gaze, her warmth. "I think so." He choked out the words.

"Then you have to try. Love like that doesn't come around very often. And you both deserve a lifetime of magic."

Chapter Twenty-Seven

"Life's pretty weird sometimes, isn't it?" Cass' sister-in-law, Annabelle, rested on her stomach, her head propped up on her hands next to Cass.

They were in Cass' basement apartment. When Cass and Nathan had lived here, the cozy, private blanket had wrapped around them. Now the darkness practically strangled her. The only good thing about her living quarters was that it sat under her brother and sister-in-law. Cass was going to need their support more than ever. "Understatement of the year."

"Your brother and I can't get pregnant no matter what we try."

There was a scar in her heart over how many miscarriages and failed invitro tries Annabelle and Garrett had suffered.

Annabelle took a sip of her wine and set it back on the bedside table. "And you." She waved her hand delicately over Cass' body. Everything Annabelle did was delicate. Even drunk she maintained her royal-like composure. Years ago, when they'd first met, Cass had silently dismissed her as flighty and weak because of her daintiness. "You, hussy, manage to wind up pregnant even with a dead husband." Annabelle dissolved into giggles. "I'm shorry, sorry. It is funny. You have to admit."

"*I'm* sorry, Annabelle. This should be you. I always wanted you guys to have a baby. I want to be an auntie almost as much as you want to be a mom."

"Hush now." Annabelle put her hand on Cass' belly. "This is nothing to be sorry about. We're going to have a baby in the family," she squealed. "I'm going to be the best goddamned auntie ever. It's the dicks who should be sorry. Dickweed weasel number one for getting you pregnant. And supreme asshole fucker dickweed number two for breaking your heart. I might have to auntie it from prison if I they ever cross my path."

Delicate was an illusion. Cass knew better now. Her sister's swearing could rival any sailor's mouth and her core was stronger than a steel vault. Not to mention, if anyone messed with someone Annabelle loved, fire and brimstone would be mild compared to the scorched earth left behind Annabelle's retribution.

"It's not either of their faults." Cass patted Annabelle's hand.

"Hello, do you need for me to explain how a baby is made? It requires a penis at some point. Apparently for you only one point. Oh! I crack myself up." Annabelle wiped her tears after laughing herself silly and finished her wine. Cass knew she'd be asleep soon. Drunk Annabelle fell quickly into passed-out Annabelle. Three glasses of wine were all it took.

"The renegade heartbreaker is the spawn of the devil. How dare he."

"Dramatic much?"

"Please, why be bland when you can be a rainbow?"

Cass thought of Lily. Perhaps that was why the woman's friendship had come so easily, because she reminded Cass of Annabelle.

"But really, I just want you to be so, so happy. You are my best friend. You're smarter than anyone I know, the world lights up around you and your heart is so fucking beautiful! I mean what the fuck is wrong with him?"

Not much. Her heart hurt from missing Adam, probably because she'd left it back there in his hands. She'd done that, then she'd run away. Now it was like her phantom limb. "I kind of shut him out, didn't really give him a chance after I found out," Cass whispered, so afraid to admit her truths.

Annabelle put her head on the pillow and faced Cass. "What? I thought you said he was mad at you?"

Cass gripped her sister-in-law's hand willing the tears to stay put inside her eyeballs. She was so fucking tired of crying.

"Honey, talk to me."

"I fell in love with him," she cried. "He's amazing, lovely, hot as hell, funny. And I thought, finally, I get to be happy again. I was careful with him, with myself around him. We took it slow because I knew I didn't want to be reckless and angry anymore. And I was afraid to love again. He was special enough to cherish. He cherished *me.* I believed my heart deserved love. It freed me, Annie, the entire place, the land, his family. I was writing again. I felt so alive, invigorated, cherished, secure. And…"

"Then you got the shock of a lifetime."

"And you should have seen his face when I told him. All his beautiful emotions closed off. Like I was a stranger. The man doesn't know a stranger. It hurt so much. He said stupid things, I said stupid things. Well, we didn't actually say that much."

"Not to excuse his behavior, but he was probably in shock too. If he fell head over heels like it sounds, then whammo!"

"I know, right." Cass laughed through her tears. "I mean the absurdity of it all!"

"Do you want to be with him still?"

Cas sighed and grabbed a tissue. She took a huge sip of orange soda Annabelle had poured into a red wine glass for her. "I don't think I can do that to him."

"Do what? Love him, give him you, the most precious gift in the world?"

"His dreams are made of wonder and belief...so much hope," she whispered. "He's so young and naïve." She wanted to make herself believe that he was naïve, but really she adored his beautiful belief in the goodness of the world, the rightness that he maintained. It was a strength he carried unlike any she'd seen before. "He wants the perfect life in the perfect land with his perfect wife who is innocent, unscarred, waiting for him to complete her world. Absolutely not someone who has as much baggage as I have, including a baby from a man I'll never be able to find. I can barely even remember what the guy looked like."

"I think you're making excuses. I think you're scared." Annabelle would give it to her straight, no doubt about it. "There's no such thing as perfect, honey. Not for any of us. You know that. And you can't decide for him what he wants. Only he can tell you. I'm perfectly fine calling him a perfectly dumb asshole farmer on his perfectly wretched land if you are *not* what he wants. But don't you want to ask him? You should take every chance you get to try to make your own happiness."

Annabelle lived what she preached, that was for sure. She'd fought to love Cass' brother Garrett even when her family said she couldn't. She'd climbed her way to being a prestigious finance professor and was trying again and again for a baby after every crushing heartbreak and disappointment. Here was bravery right in front of Cass, bold and unashamed.

"What do I do?" God, she sounded so weak. She was afraid.

"What are your dreams, honey? What do you want? Do you want to try and work things out with him?"

She nodded. "I feel so old and tired, too jaded to believe, but I want to try."

"If you're old, I'm halfway in my grave already."

"Please, you're barely two years older than me."

"Two years and fifteen days to be exact. Older *and* wiser, don't forget. And I'll tell you what *I* want. I want you to wrap things up here, whatever it is you came back for anyway, other than to hide. Go get your sexy farmer. We all need a sexy farmer."

"Hey now, settle down."

"I'm teasing." Annabelle yawned. "I want you to have a big, beautiful wedding with your hottie. Then I'm going to throw you the biggest fucking baby shower in the world."

"I don't think we use 'fucking' in the same sentence as 'baby shower'."

"You do if you're a badass like me," Annabelle said and dragged herself up. "I need to go upstairs and find my sexy surgeon so he can kiss me before I fall asleep. He's such a good kisser, the way he—"

"Go! Too much information, lady."

Annabelle kissed her forehead. "Love you, Cassie."

"Love you back, Annie."

Right before she walked out, she turned and said, "I might not believe in perfect, honey, but I do believe in magic."

Despite her fatigue, Cass didn't sleep much. She snuggled into her pillow and conjured dreams of love and tried to untangle the mysteries of the heart.

Chapter Twenty-Eight

Adam walked the last few blocks to the address he had for her apartment. The city was cold and damp and overgrown with concrete, a solid gray cage tightening its bars around him. He didn't know how anyone would want to live here. No grass, no fields. He had yet to see a tree. Noise and movement and people were everywhere, busy, rushed, unknown. It took him half an hour to wedge his truck into the tiniest parking space possible. And pay for it. Who fucking paid to park? No one in Graciella, that was who.

Pieces of garbage were stuck to the wet pavement and a man slept in a doorway under a blanket. It startled him at first, then sank his heart. Adam couldn't simply walk by and do nothing. He slipped some cash into the hand holding tight to a weathered and worn blanket.

Bleak, depressing, loud. Maybe he'd made a mistake coming here, if this was where she wanted to be, in an overcrowded city with people and garbage strewn as if they were the same thing.

He turned the corner into a spicy garlic scent that smacked him in the face, and his stomach rumbled. A Thai restaurant with a line of people waiting in its warm entry. A few storefronts down, a tiny wine bar where people snuggled together at a bar, lit with low lighting. *Romantic.* A woman threw back her head and laughed. Distracted, he nearly bumped into two men holding hands, one with his arms full of takeout. All these delicious cuisines wrapped around him, along with people enjoying life, connected, being wooed.

There's more to her city than concrete and garbage.

Coffee and cereal had lost their appeal to Adam days ago, but it was what he'd survived on, barely even tasting either. Now walking past restaurant after restaurant and late-night coffee shops with people touching and smiling and eating food that smelled so amazing it had him drooling, he had an inkling of why Cass, food writer extraordinaire, would want to live here. *How difficult it must have been to be here when she lost her sense of smell.* The city-wide food scene must be incredible if this was only an inch of it.

It warped his stride, nearly made him stop completely. Christ, he couldn't even cook for her. And how could he offer her dreams of food writing in Graciella? There were only so many ways she could spin the barn dinners at Brockman House, or a croissant from Marigold Bakery. She'd have a handful of essays to write at best.

He let the surroundings, alive in the night, guide his way in the darkness. Like the farm in a way, not all of it was lovely. But this place, made him feel colder. There were no real stars here, all had been snuffed out by manmade shiny. He felt untethered from the land, from the sky, the stars, the water. There was too much in the way of it all.

By the time he stood at the bottom set of steps leading up to a stately, old three-story home, he was stiff. Anxiety churned in his gut. He'd been so damn certain coming here, following his heart, his everything. But Cass was more sophisticated than this city. Would a simple farm life be enough for her?

"Adam?" Jesus Christ, her voice. He could breathe again.

"Is that him? The one who got you pregnant and disappeared?" The man with Cass got in his face ready to spar, anger rolling off him in waves.

"Garrett, stop! That's not him." Cass shoved her way between them. "Adam, what are you doing here?"

Like he wouldn't travel the world to find her. Now his heart started again, wanted to leap out of his chest and grab hold of her. *And never let her go again.*

"I came for you. I mean I came…to talk —"

"Oh," she said. One simple word, but he couldn't tell if it held hope or resistance.

"Shit. Sorry, man. I'm Garret, Cass' brother." He held out his hand. "It appears Cass has more secrets." The resemblance between them was there, in the eyes. But where Garret's were clear, healthy, assessing, his Cass looked exhausted and her hollow eyes gazed at him like she couldn't believe he was there. Did she want him to be, or not? *Fuck.* Again, he hadn't taken into consideration her feelings. He should have called, but he hated the phone and he needed her by his side in order to breathe.

"I told you about Adam." She shooed her brother away.

Even with her bossy tone, warmth and ease flowed between the siblings.

"You didn't tell me he was madly in love with you," Garret said and nudged her. "I'll uh, be inside. Hope to catch you later."

Adam hadn't taken his eyes off Cass and her gaze widened at Garret's words.

"Hi," he said.

There she was, warmth and beauty and love and his. He longed to enfold her, but nerves glued his words in his throat and his body to the pavement.

She made no move either. Would it be like this now, this awkward unrecognizable vastness between them?

"I owe you a huge apology," he said and followed his heart. He stepped into her and took her hand. His need to be connected won out over any sanity in the moment. "I'm so sorry, Cassandra."

"I'm the one who left," she said in a tired voice. "I was in shock, hurting, and I pushed you away. I left without saying goodbye. I was so scared. I'm still scared."

He shook his head. "I made your pain, what you were going through, about me. I never meant to scare you."

"No." She put her fingers over his lips. "I wasn't afraid of you. I'm scared to death to have a baby and I'm scared by…my feelings for you, by this enormous everything between us."

"Yeah." Adam wrapped her in his arms. She sighed and settled into him. It was more than he deserved.

"I came to explain my stupidity. I'll go if that's what you want, but I'm begging you to let me try again."

The tiny hint of smile gave him the courage he needed to continue. Damn she felt good in his arms. She wrapped hers around him and held on. *Thank God.*

"When you told me what had happened, and I acted like a jerk, it wasn't you I was pissed at or thought less of. I'm so sorry I made you feel ashamed. It was him, whoever he is, that I was angry at, because as your brother noticed, I am madly in love with you and I couldn't understand how any man wouldn't want you to be his forever. I could never do just one night with you... I'm so in love with you it hurts."

She ran her hands over his face, gently. It was the soothing he'd been missing his entire life. Clasping her hands to his face, he drank his fill of her. Then he put his entire heart and dreams out there for her.

"I want to be your forever. Come back to Graciella with me, to Brockman Farms. Make a life with me, you and the baby. Be my forever."

Chapter Twenty-Nine

Nothing lasts forever. "There's no such thing." Words spilled out in a jumbled mess. He'd just confessed his love for her, and she'd alluded to the same. Maybe she couldn't do this. Maybe she wasn't brave like the Annabelles and the Adams of the world. It was why she'd hurried away from Brockman Farms like a mouse scurrying under cover. *Running. Hiding.*

He deserved to have his dreams with someone free, someone as strong as he was. She barely believed in next month. Here she'd found someone wonderful, but she wouldn't be able to have him. They were too different. All her insecurities bled into each other.

"I can't do that to you, can't ask you to take on my burdens, to accept less than what you deserve. I know your dreams. I don't even have a job, a way to support myself and this bean growing inside me." She held tight to his jacket and pleaded. For him to understand? Or smash all her excuses into smithereens?

"You and a baby are not burdens, not *less*." He cupped her face in his rough, strong hands that always held her as though she were precious. "You're both a gift. You are my dream. You walked into my life and catapulted me into the sky from the first moment. My dream is to cherish you, hear you laugh, make love to you, find creative ways to woo you because my cooking skills suck, grow old with you. I want to take care of you, not because you can't take care of yourself, but because it's who I am."

She leaned into his chest at his easy, honest statements. "How can you be so idealistic? So true and grounded and certain? Won't you regret it, regret *me* eventually? I couldn't bear that, Adam. You treat me like I'm the most meaningful beautiful thing you've ever discovered, and it might kill me to have that change."

When she braved his look, she saw she hadn't even fazed him. Nothing she said had deterred him. How could a man be so hopeful, so stalwart? His smile was wide, assured, his eyes connected and intense, the way they always were. She wanted to borrow his confidence.

"My father died last year. You know that."

"Yes," she said and gave him a squeeze. There were so many serious issues they'd never spoken of.

"He was a spiteful, nasty man. Dirty in the worst ways. I knew early on I was nothing to him. Avoided him as much as I could. It helped having Cruz and Turner there when we were boys. When I was fifteen, Katie left him and married Javier. For the first half of my life, I had no father...none I would claim, at least. For the past twelve, almost thirteen years, Javier has been a father to me, a real one. He taught me, listened to me, guided me back from stupidville many a time. I recognize his love as sure as if he were my own father. He is my father. The only one I know. He reminded me recently of the importance of choosing our family, which is stronger than blood sometimes. He taught me that. I've tried to be like him to walk in his shadow. I want you and this baby to be my family."

Swatting all her apprehension away, he made her heart unfurl, peek out, begin to emerge.

"I know I'll screw some things up. But I will *never* think of you with anything but joy, reverence, desire. You are my star. There might not be such a thing as forever. Then be my everything. Be my today. We'll hope for lots of tomorrows. We can always have hope. I want as many days as I can have with you by my side. Let me love you. Make a family with me."

Could she do that? Maybe that was what frightened her the most, this unique bond she had with him unlike any she'd had with another human. Powerful and fragile at the same time. All of that scared the hell out of her. But maybe it was okay to be scared in the safety of his arms. Arms that cared for every living thing around him.

"I don't think you walk in his shadow, Javier's. I think you walk beside him. You are the most remarkable man I know and you should be proud."

And when he kissed her, he set her heart free. He kissed his love into her, his strength, his hope.

"What about your dreams?" he asked under the foggy moonlight. "What do you want?"

"To not fall asleep every five seconds." One dream had been her constant. "I want to write. It's my passion. I found it again at your farm. Weeks ago, I still wanted my job at the paper back, but I'm not sure. That seems like such a distant journey in my past. Especially now that I'm pregnant. Food and writing combined in some delicious way, but I'm still figuring out what that means in the form of a career. Your farm has me bursting with inspiration, though." She tossed her head back. "I could write an entire book on Miranda's croissants alone."

"I want you to have and be and do whatever you want. Selfishly, I want you to be with me."

"I want you too. You gave me back my dreams. You give me the possibility of new dreams."

They stood holding each other, taking strength from each other, sharing warmth and love and secrets in the silence.

"I can't believe you came all this way," Cass said. She took his face and kissed him. "I missed you so much. I wanted to call you every day. I ran away basically. Well, I told myself the responsible thing to do would be to come home. I'd intended to try to find the man I was with that stupid night, which turned out to be an empty search. What kind of mother am I going to be? I've already screwed up so royally right from the beginning."

"You didn't screw up. I think love is a pretty good place to start. And your love is magnificent." He absolutely melted her into a pile of mushy emotions. She didn't even bother to wipe her tears. They were on autopilot these days.

He lowered his forehead to hers. "When you left, my heart stopped. Your love was gone. I was angry at myself, for being a selfish ass. Christ, I haven't even asked you how you're doing." Adam pulled back to fix his intense study upon her. "I didn't even ask you that morning, how you were feeling, your body, falling off a horse, being pregnant."

"I'm good, constantly hungry," she said and they both laughed. "Honestly, I think I'm still in disbelief. Still napping like a gold medal winner. The doctors say everything is fine. We're both healthy, mama and baby." The jagged sigh Adam let out betrayed how worried he'd been.

"I missed you too." She wrapped her arms around him and soothed him the way he always did her. A strong man could be afraid. She knew that now. She wanted to know and care for him the way he cared for her.

"Come home with me, darlin'?" he asked and she smiled into his neck.

"First you need to come in and meet my brother, properly, and my sister-in-law."

"I'm not going to get punched, am I?"

"No," Cass laughed. "Annabelle is more likely to drop kick you down and strangle you until you promise to take good care of me."

"I think I can take it."

"We're going to need to build that house of yours," she said. The chilly night swirled around them, but she could spend every moment she had left right here in the sidewalk wrapped in his arms.

"House of ours," he said. "With an office fit for a writer. And a nursery."

Chapter Thirty

If the bitter wind didn't knock him down and pummel him first, Adam might actually make it to the cottage without any more bruises for the day. It whipped around in a mad frenzy, screeching out its fury, and it was fucking *cold*. So cold he could hardly get a breath. His eyeballs hurt from the shrill negative temps. His fingers were frozen through and the farm sagged like some shriveled dystopian wasteland streaked with gray and white, washed of all color. His boots crunched across the thin layer of ice and dirt on the walk to Cass.

Lovely, brilliant, warm Cassandra. Mine.

Images of Cassandra's lush, curvy, growing body heated him, conquering the wicked gale that tried to take him down. Bullet beat him to the cottage and waited, huddled over against the wind.

"Come on, boy, let's get warm." Adam let them both in. Bullet shot right to his bed by the fire, pawed at his cushion as if it had wounded him, grabbed the sock toy

Cass had given him and slumped into a pile of contented fur.

"Ahh," Adam sighed. He loved winter now. When he entered the cottage and hefted the door shut behind him, blocking out all the angry frozen fingers of January, it was like stepping from the apocalypse into a magical heaven, and most recently a pizza heaven.

The soothing warmth from the gas fireplace wrapped around him like a friendly ghost, cracked his shell and allowed him to relax. Lingering aromas of sautéed onions, garlic and tomatoes hit his nose along with the hint of rising yeasty dough. She must have made more sauce this morning. It was a pizzeria all right. Cass had moved from craving icy orange sodas to pizza.

It had to be a certain dough — good thing she knew how to make it — only one kind of sauce — her mother's recipe, rich and tomatoey — the exact right kind of cheese and toppings. Adam wasn't complaining. All of it was the best pizza he'd ever had. Any of them had ever had. Lily and Miranda were already planning to build a pizza oven on the farm for the barn dinners.

Last night, she'd tried to teach him how to make dough. It had been all well and good until they'd come to the kneading. Their bodies close, her hands on his showing him how to knead, how to push and pull and gather. He'd gotten distracted by her neck. The next thing he'd known, they were on the floor naked and she'd been riding him. It had gone from well and good to earth-shattering in a matter of minutes. He grinned. Adam could say with absolute certainty that his first cooking lesson had gone stupendously.

"Cass," he called. "Darlin'?" When she didn't answer, he smiled. *Good, I didn't miss her morning nap.*

Adam peeled himself out from under layers — coat, sweater, hat, gloves and boots — shedding pounds as he did it, and went in search of his darlin'.

Oh yeah, winter might have quickly become his favorite season.

He stood at the doorway to her bedroom. Weak winter sunlight filtered through the gauzy curtains and over her body snuggled under the down comforter. All he could see was the soft skin of her cheeks and honey hair flowing out around her.

"Hi," she said, without opening her eyes. Her smile called to him. Still sleepy, she patted the bed next to her. "I missed you."

"I was only gone a few hours." Most of. which she had probably slept through.

"I know," she said like he'd been gone two years. Even still lost in the hazy remains of sleep, she could pout. Gorgeous, eyes closed, curled into a cozy shape, her anxiety smoothed out. No fear or concerns furrowed her brow. He watched her closely, his concern for her and the baby a living, untamed beast in his chest these days.

Waking hours, she *was* worried, and scared. She'd admitted as much to him. And who wouldn't be carrying a child. Life-changing plans forcing her to acknowledge them. No job — although he didn't give a hoot about that and would take care of her, of them, like he'd promised. He got it, the need to support herself and her child, but he didn't want her overstressed. It nicked at the back of his mind when he was near, and especially when he wasn't by her side.

She was also brave and strong. *And warm.* That brought a smile to his face. He quickly shed his jeans and shirt and climbed in next to her, dragging the covers back over them. *Talk about dreams.* She was always warm and dewy, his own personal fire, after taking care of the animals in this frigid season. Horses and cows didn't hibernate, and their hungry stomachs and needs waited for no stupid man.

"Oh! Your feet are freezing!" Her sleepy smiling voice nuzzled in against his neck as she stretched her limbs and cuddled back in.

"Mmm." He mimicked her snuggle and wrapped his hands around her to pull them as close as they could get, bodies flush together, legs tangled. "You're my furnace." Her body had taken on the scents of dough and yeast. He breathed in deeply.

"I can't believe you faced the outside in this nasty weather."

He kissed her soft lips. "I'm never leaving again. You are every good and sinful thing in this world." His hands roamed then, taking on a mind of their own with desire, over skin, over curves, over soft fabric, the arch of her back, her ass he loved especially and her wide hips. Clean sheets mixed with the yeast and her underlying seductive flower scent. He could be rolling in the warm summer field of flowers with her even in the darkest days of winter. That was what she did to him, for him, seduced his entire world into love and light and summer warmth. *She* took away all his fears and he wanted to do the same for her, out of bed and in.

"Forget the farm, forget the animals. I'm staying right here forever." He sighed with pleasure as her body heated his. The cold might have tried to douse his libido, but with one touch—hell with a *smile*—she stirred his blood to boiling and had him hard and needy. Seconds, it took. The power she had over him.

"You definitely have something with this whole forever thing." She wiggled into him, her lush body covered only in a thin tank top and some taunting lacy underwear covering the hips he wanted access to. Teasing his fingers under them, he finally got what he wanted, what he needed, what he craved — a hand full of her naked secret curves, all soft and lush in his palm. He loved their forevers now. Their daily inside jokes about forever foot rubs and forever naps and forever making love. Forever had a whole new meaning for them both. It was whatever they wanted it to mean. It was a tangible, wondrous thing they grabbed on to at every chance.

"Adam," she huffed, impatient now, and used her legs to help his hands divest her of the pretty but frustratingly in-his-way lace. He tossed it over his shoulder and she laughed deep and sexy, her voice still halfway in dreamland. He took her laugh with a kiss, searing and hungry. Cass dragged herself away and impatiently shrugged out of her tank, sighing in pleasure as their bodies met again.

"You have so many clothes on," she said, lost and lingering in her lazy waking phase, eyes still closed, smile luring and seductive body all arching curves and taut muscles. His sleek jungle cat.

"Boxers are *so* many?" He smiled as he nipped her neck, her shoulders, famished for all of her.

"Anything is too many. I dreamed of you. I'm always dreaming of you when you're gone." It was both a whimper and a greedy cherishing. Now her expression shone with knowledge, of erotic dreams she didn't want to be woken from. Adam aimed to make those dreams a reality for both of them.

"What did you dream about, Cassandra?" He dragged himself lower, palming and kneading her skin. Oh, he knew how to knead all right. He kissed and nipped at her on his way down, her hardened dark nipples a salve for his starving mouth, her aching cries and writhing body his reward. He gently rubbed his lips over her hardening belly, the smallest of bumps growing there and whispered words of love and peace. She sucked in a breath when he made it even lower, to the deepest core of her where her clit was so swollen and needy for him. He teased with his tongue, a lick, a kiss, before he took her in his mouth, sucking and eating at her inner heat.

"It's too much," she moaned and gripped his head, the scrape of her fingers through his scalp one more stroke to his fire. "So good and too much. How can I be…" Her breath caught again at his hungry assault, his gentle kisses. "How can I be so needy all the time for you? I ache for you. Constantly on the edge. And in my dreams, it's even stronger, like a drug. Better than any… Adam!" And she splintered apart in his mouth, crying out her release in his name. "Adam, Adam, Adam. Come here. I need you. I need you inside me." Her breath was heavy, panting.

Every day he discovered new things about her. An old scar on her hip that he kissed on his journey back up. That she craved coffee with an angry vengeance, but couldn't stand the smell of it once it reached her nose these days. How cranky it made her when a recipe didn't turn out. How she sang to him in the bathtub and it was the most beautiful sound. The flush on her chest when she came. A kiss there too. That tears came to her in happiness as easily as sadness. How bossy she was when her needy body craved his. She could boss him around all the time.

Impatient now, Cass pulled at him, hooked her slender feet into the rim of his boxers, trying to nudge them off. His demanding beauty. His impatience matched hers and again he was grateful that both his and Cass' testing had come back clean and they could do away with condoms. He made quick work of the boxers and, tucking himself back next to her, he slipped inside her wet slick heat, still pulsing from the onslaught of his mouth.

Fuck! She gripped him there and pulsed around him, even while she threw her head back and cried out her pleasure, which made him harder with aching. He slowed his pace to prolong the delicious agony, thrusting in and out of her slowly, drowning in her heat while he joined their mouths and tugged her leg over his hips so he could go deeper and feel all of her wrapped around him, all her power taking his, taking him and guiding him into the sweet, sweet warmth of her oblivion.

Chapter Thirty-One

Cass stretched out her sleepy warm body and opened her eyes to the fading sunlight. What a gorgeous time of day, especially with her love next to her. "Hi," she said, and got to watch his sexy, knowing smile spread across his face.

Memories of *her* earlier "Hi" when he'd come home flushed her entire body. Her sexy, tender farmer lit a fuse in her sexual desires. Insatiable didn't begin to describe her, and she didn't give one hoot if it had anything to do with being pregnant and hormones. Actually, she did. She'd like to write a long and passionate thank you to pregnancy hormones and desire. There should be an encyclopedia, an entire dissertation on the topic.

"Afternoon, beauty." Her entire body flushed under the caress of his words, the rough sound of his voice and the way he always caused a fluttering inside her. The way his eyes sought out her truth. Every time. It might have been disconcerting if she didn't feel the same about him and want to open herself fully to his love.

"Oh my goodness." She propped herself up on her elbow and reached a finger to his cheek. "What happened? I can't believe I didn't notice this earlier."

"Perfectly okay with the way you didn't notice it earlier," he teased. "Lost in your dreamland is one of my favorite positions with you."

"Lost in my dreamland, huh?"

"Mmm, my new favorite place to travel. I'm going to get a passport so I can go anytime I want. You make a delicious tour guide." He snuggled his face into her chest, and she had to use all her will power not to succumb to his seduction.

"Did you get in another fight with your brothers?" A dark bruise blossomed and swelled under his right eye.

They'd talked for hours in his truck on the drive back from San Francisco. Told each other details of the days they'd been apart. Talked about favorite foods and movies. They'd barely skated the edge of family dynamics. She'd had momming and babies on her brain, but when she'd asked him about his childhood he'd joked and changed the subject. It was the first time he'd evaded talking about his family. He had shared a bit about his argument with Cruz and Turner and how they'd sort of cleared the air, but she suspected there was more to the story, dusty leftovers of hurt.

Cruz and Turner always behaved like really good guys, but essentially, they'd left him. And so had she. And every time someone left him, it bruised his beautiful soul. He was extremely good at hiding those emotions, covering them with his humor and bold, friendly confidence. And his strength.

"No, darlin'." Adam laughed. "The day one of them gets in this good of a shot on me, you can put me in my grave. Besides, we don't get physical when we're really angry with each other. All that rolling around is teasing and one-upping, playing. Silver Ghost did this. Got my jaw too."

"Silver Ghost?" She raised her eyebrow and gave a gentle brush to his jaw. There was no bruise there.

"New rescue horse. Poor girl is starving and pissed off. I'd be too if someone took horrible care of me, then abandoned me to the winter. Clocked me in the head twice before I moved away. Got a lot of hidden strength left in her, which is a great sign."

"Only you would consider being hit in the head twice by a horse a great sign."

"Strength means she'll be okay. Didn't let the bad stuff break her soul. That's all I need to help her heal."

"You're good at taking care of broken things." Cass wrapped her arms around him. *Abandoned.* Her heart ached with the realization. He'd channeled his own wounds into caring for other creatures who suffered the same lot.

"I've always loved taking care of the animals. Eventually they let their guards down and trust me back. It's powerful."

And probably filled all the cracks of his own soul that had been abused or treated poorly, that had been left behind. Trust was such a delicate thing between humans and animals, from human to human.

"I'm sorry I left," she said and placed a hand on his heart. She kept her gaze locked on his. "I'm sorry I left you. It was a rash decision based on fear and I hurt you."

"Darlin'." One word in his deep, soft voice spoke more than any other flowery things he could have said. Somehow without her even apologizing, he'd already forgiven her.

"Why did your brothers go so far away for so long?"

He cradled her ass with his large caring hand and fingered her hair with the other. One of her new favorite positions, snuggled in as close as she could get, held to him. She wanted the emotional too, hoping he'd open up and give it to her. She wanted to earn that same level of trust from him, make him realize he could lean on her too, tell her all his past sadness, his fears. Assure him she'd never abandon him again. His heart was full of strength, but that didn't mean it wasn't precious too.

"Because T.D. was a complete bastard. That's pretty much all there was to him, unless you count intelligent and cunning, a lethal combination."

Oh no. No.

"I was the scrawny runt of the litter and always on his radar to mock. Loved by my mom and brothers, I didn't bond with him like Turner did at first, which is his damage to deal with. T.D. was a bully I tried to ignore. When he got really mean, I had two older brothers to protect me." Adam's grip on her tightened.

"Honey," she prodded.

When he met her eyes again, his sky-blue ones were full of anguish. "I just fucking realized how bad it must have been for them, for Cruz and Turner." Adam shook his head. To try to make sense of the knowledge, or toss it away? She couldn't be sure.

"Hey, come back to me. Talk to me. I want to take care of you too."

He sucked in a breath and relaxed into their cocoon again.

"I don't think I ever took into account what life was like for either of them. T.D. hated Cruz because my mom was already pregnant with him when she was forced to marry T.D. And in a sick way, he tried to mold Turner into his likeness. My brothers protected me from all of that. Suddenly they were gone, pretty close on the heels of each other, and we left Brockman House to live with Javier. Best moment of my life, and also the worst. I was fifteen going on know-it-all twenty-five. Pissed at the world."

"Because of T.D.?"

"Not as you'd think. It was the loss, the changes. I lost my brothers, but it was losing the land, Brockman Farms, family land, *my* land. It felt like someone had stripped my lungs from my body. Logically I was happy for my mom, and relieved to be away from T.D., but I couldn't comprehend losing all of it. The farm was my heart."

Cass imagined a teenage Adam, gangly, freckles, wild hair, all pissed off about having to leave his farm behind. *I wonder if he was as big and strong then, this gentle giant too big in body and mind for the cruel, confusing people of the world.* He was so tender and vulnerable even as a grown-up. She ran her hands over his head and through his thick hair and watched him close his eyes and sigh with a dreamy expression as he settled into her touch. *Like one of his wild horses gentling under a loving caress.*

"I was stomping around our new house, huffing at everyone like an angry stallion who wasn't allowed to run."

"I can picture it."

He kissed her throat and she could feel from such a simple gesture more anger seep out of him.

"Bet you were pretty cute, though?"

He looked at her like she was crazy. "I was a fucking mess. Skin and ridiculously long bones. Scrawny, uncoordinated unless I was riding a horse, my voice was late to change and I had terrible acne. Christ, I hurt from growing. I shot up at least six inches that year, but it took me another two years to bulk out. Everything made me angry. Mom tossed me right in therapy."

"*You*?" No man in Cassandra's life had ever gone to therapy. Even Nathan had rolled his eyes about mental health.

"For three years. Roxanna had gone, my mother went and she knew I needed someone to help me deal with all my wacky emotions and hormones. She was right as usual. In the beginning, it was one more thing that pissed me off. I was indignant, affronted, but Dr. Cook was pretty cool and it began to lessen the pressure in my chest to talk to someone who could help me work out my anger. He basically had to beat down my brick wall, because like all self-important idiots, I didn't need to *handle* my emotions. But once he did, it was like this tightness around my chest loosened."

Cass hadn't gone when Nathan died. And it hit her then, even through her smile and happiness and relaxed warmth, that parts of her wounds were merely still covered over in brambles. They hadn't had a chance to heal. So many emotions at the same time smacked into her.

"Hey, now, why the tears?" Adam wiped them away and held her face in his hands.

"It's selfish. I don't want to make this about me. We're talking about you."

"I don't find you crying and wanting to join in the conversation selfish. Tell me."

"I think maybe I should talk to someone." Her words were a whisper. She laughed through her tears. "I mean, I know I need to."

"Did you go after your husband died?"

She shook her head and reached beside the bed for tissues. "I suppressed a lot of my grief, shut it all away. And now my hormones are all wonky and unpredictable."

"There are some good doctors here in Graciella. I can help you find one if you want."

"I think I'd like that." She swallowed down her emotions and leaned into him. "I don't want you to think I'm still devastated over his death, like I'm pining for Nathan, wishing him back, that I can't love again. I mean I will always love him, miss him. But I really did bury my grief and with all this" — she rubbed her belly — "my body's even more out of control. Things are seeping out all over the place. I don't want to be a blubbering, confused mess all the time. If my big, sexy farmer can take care of his mental health, so can I."

"What can I do to help?"

"Tell me more about young Adam when his world turned upside down."

"You know, stories of surly teenage Adam kind of go against my whole plan to dazzle you."

Dazzle. "No worries there," she said. He'd brought love into her life again, sparkly, life-affirming love. How could he not know how much he enchanted her every day? Safe within his arms, she could fall apart and he'd catch her. He had over and over again. And he made her feel so many things. His hands rubbed her back and with her front pressed up against his, all kinds of sensations brushed away her sad for now.

"Prepare," he said and puffed out his chest, mocking himself in that silly way.

"I think I can handle it." Cass squeezed his biceps and got a grin out of him.

"Right around when I turned seventeen, I had another huge growth spurt. Several inches in a few months and fifty pounds. More inches later. I kept growing, was hungry all the time, hated school, and I was obsessed with—"

"Girls?" she guessed, pinching his side. *Bet they were obsessed with you too, and the boys. A young, handsome, built Adam Brockman with his charming grin and twinkly blue eyes? Everyone probably drooled over him.*

"Horses," he said, swatting her hand away and capturing it in his, fake affronted at her insinuation. "Everything else was a distraction I couldn't be bothered with. Not girls, not showering, not cleaning my room. I was moon-eyed for them. Nothing else mattered to my young heart. I was pitiful."

She laughed at his description. He really was like a little kid with his favorite toys whenever he talked about or was around horses. And honestly, tucked into his arms under soft blankets while the world quieted in winter around them, she could listen to him talk about horses all day. His rumbly voice and closeness and complete openness with her, no qualms, complete humility. Such a comforting and sexy combination, especially the way his voice tuned all the right notes inside her, sending flitters of anticipation coursing through her. She rubbed against him.

"Now I'm distracted by another kind of beauty."

"You are, huh?"

"Mmm-hmm. I'm distracted by your eyes." He kissed one, then the other. "By your skin right here on your neck." His lips soothed and tingled at the same time, and her breaths came shorter as his large, capable, delicious hands roamed down her back and kneaded her butt.

"Oh." She moaned her admiration. "Honey, I love it when you touch me like that, but we have a more important issue. Like serious, immediate, needs to be seen to now."

"We do?" Adam kissed her neck again. But she untangled herself from his embrace and sat up, throwing her legs over the side of the bed.

"I'm starving." She felt him pause. Then it was his turn to burst out laughing.

Chapter Thirty-Two

How had she ever believed him too young? He was the strongest, most dynamic man she knew. His naivete was a ruse or perhaps one tiny layer of him, because he was also constantly learning. His quiet open adoration for the world, the way he listened and took note of everything wasn't naïve. It was refreshing and humble. It most likely gave him the edge he had with the horses too. A special bond with the equine beasts.

"Hey, girl. You like that sunshine, don't you," Adam said.

It had been almost a month since he'd gotten ownership of Silver Ghost. Cass didn't think there could be a horse as stunning as Gracie, but Sylvie, as Adam had nicknamed her, was a close second. And the change in her from when she arrived at Brockman Farms till now was unbelievable.

Sylvie's ears tweaked at the sound of Adam's gentle voice, the only indication she'd heard him. She didn't lift her head from the hay or make any move to come closer. She was in the paddock near Cass' cottage, which was more secluded and away from much of the barns and all their noise and business, where Cass had watched Adam and Gracie that special night months ago.

The mare stood speckled in gray and white, much of her back covered in a blanket, in the only patch of dappled sunlight. Cass hugged her oversized sweater around her and was grateful for the wool hat and mittens Katie had given her, because the sun was out today, thank goodness, but in the shade, they were still under winter's freezing grip.

"Got a treat for you, darlin'." Adam winked at Cass, but spoke to Sylvie. That man and his darlin's could have her melted into a puddle of lust even in the freezing temps.

There he was, working his sorcery on one more wounded creature. *Wizard of wild things, my tender, patient, sexy man.* If the state of Sylvie's coat, her healing leg and that near smile on her face when Adam spoke to her was any indication, his magic was working.

Sylvie still wasn't keen on much touching. Only Adam could get close. But Cass cheered when the mare took the apple from Adam's palm, then nuzzled his empty hand for more. Trust was being built day by day, gesture by gesture.

Cass was trying to do the same with Adam. Even though he'd said he wasn't hurt by her leaving, she saw his vulnerable heart and it brought her so much joy to care for it with actions and words to build his trust in her the way she trusted him. She didn't have any apples to offer, so she cooked for him instead. And he drooled over her food, her pizza, her brownies, especially her *sonhos*. Dreams. He was her dream. Since she'd set foot on his land, he'd captured her in his secret spell of worship and love.

When he backed away from Sylvie, she called out, "Hey, sexy farmer! Got a treat for you, darlin'." He laughed and jogged in her direction. Cass' heart settled and rallied at the same time. More love every day, a baby, maybe marriage soon. *I get to watch his joy chase me for forever.*

She was flush and curvy and glowing in the chilly winter day. She made his days. His heart stood at attention every time he saw her. He jumped the fence and vaulted over the railing to her porch and lifted her in a gentle bear hug.

"Ahh, my favorite treat in the whole world." Adam set the bag down and took her lips. "Mmm, favorite sugary, sweet goodness." He smiled against her lips when she giggled.

"You don't even know what's in the bag, silly."

"Your *sonhos*. I can smell them. And they are dynamite, but my preference is right here, Cassandra. How was your appointment?" Cass had found a therapist and was going to sessions on Tuesday mornings now. He'd offered to drive her, but she'd shooed him away to his duties and said he could drive her when she got too round to reach the steering wheel. He'd agreed only on one condition—that she let him also drive her to her baby appointments, because he wanted to be involved in every step.

She'd cried when he'd said that. Luckily, he was beginning to understand the difference between her happy tears and ones of sorrow.

"Good, honey. I like Dr. Blue. She's smart and no nonsense, a fabulous listener. It's hard sometimes to dig out the mess I'd let my emotions become, but it's freeing too. I'm still scared to death to be a mom, but I'm going to use the things she's teaching me. It's a relief, talking with someone about my fears rather than waiting until this baby is here."

Adam leaned down and kissed her belly, then snaked his hands under her sweater and tugged her close. His brothers lovingly teased him, called him love-sick for how much he wanted to be near her, always connected. *Best thing in the world to be teased about.*

"Can I share a secret, darlin'?" he whispered.

"Anything." She placed a kiss on his heart over his jacket.

"I'm scared too. I bet all new parents are."

The look of *what the heck are you smoking?* on her face was so cute he laughed.

"You?"

"Love is scary," he said and took her weight gladly when she melted into him and shone that gorgeous smile of understanding all over him, bathing him in her light. "But it sure as hell is worth it, don't you think?" He could note the ways she said *I love you* without actually saying the words yet. And damn, he couldn't wait to hear her voice them aloud. Well, he could wait—he would do anything for her, give her all the time in the world, but when she did say them, it was a moment he'd cherish.

"One more being you've rescued."

"What's that?" He quirked his grin at her.

"Bullet, Gracie, Sylvie, God knows how many other horses, me."

He wanted to rescue her right into bed, strip away all the layers of winter, make their own fire under the covers. But he had chores. Adam nuzzled into her neck, the spot right above her collarbone that drove her crazy. "You rescued me too, my sweet Cassandra. Thought my world was perfect, then you came along and tilted it. Best damn feeling ever."

Chapter Thirty-Three

So many things were growing through the winter, reaching toward spring. Cass' belly, for one. Tight and round, it was at the point where writing at a desk was starting to be awkward. Sleep had mostly disappeared, including all her languid naps, although enjoying those lazy hours with Adam in her bed, or her shower, or on the floor more than made up for the lack of zzzzs. Her hunger had grown like a vine from Jack and the Beanstalk — insatiable. A new house, full of potential in its skeletal framed state, changed daily. Her love for Adam, if such a thing was able to increase, swelled in her heart like its own new life growing.

And her creativity. Here it was, almost finished, a polished proposal she intended to send to her old boss at *The Chronicle* and an agent friend who specialized in creative non-fiction and cookbooks. Cass finished printing the last few pages and added them to the stack beside her on the modern desk Adam had built for her out of pine with metal legs and a shelf underneath.

He'd placed it in the guesthouse, along with the most comfortable cushiony pink velvet writing chair she'd ever had the pleasure of sinking into.

"Temporary" he'd said, until their house was finished. Then he'd move both into the writing room he and Lily had designed for her. She was letting them surprise her with it. All she'd requested were tons of light, space enough for an extra table next to her desk so she could spread out all her notes, and bookshelves. *Lots and lots of bookshelves.*

Cass couldn't wait till their house was completed, but she was also going to miss this special cozy cottage. It had brought her back to life. Rubbing her belly, she smiled. *I guess many things brought me back to life.* But the memories she'd made here in recuperating, with Adam, even with their goofball, Bullet, who currently slept curled up on her feet like her own personal foot heater, would always hold a precious spot in her heart.

One more thing Adam had helped her come to understand, that memories didn't have to be stored away in the dark. Her heart, his heart...they had endless space for love and remembering and honoring emotions and memories that had come before, and even more space for what was to come.

Patting the stack of pages beside her, Cass didn't know whether to vomit or give herself a smacking high-five. Both most likely. Banishing feelings of imposter syndrome and anxiety over the quality of her writing were towering craggy mountains to climb. She almost hadn't printed the pages out. Her column had never been like this. Confident, sometimes, annoyed and angry, excited had been the emotions running through her when she'd submitted her restaurant reviews and essays about food in San Francisco.

And now she was hungry again. "Come on, softy." Cass nudged Bullet awake, all eighty pounds and still growing of him. It was a challenge to see if she or Bullet ate more these days. "Let's get a snack." He shot up and into the kitchen, plopped his butt down and paw up, waiting impatiently, but cutely for his soup bone. He definitely knew the word *snack*.

This collection of essays she'd almost completed was huge, not only in word count compared to her weekly one thousand-word columns, but in emotion. Her entire heart was in this manuscript proposal. Because it wasn't just about food and how it tasted. It was about sensual, delicious, exploratory, learning nature of food. It was about love, some grief, a dusting of magic, life, renewal, connection and comfort. It was definitely chock-full of story, an element that she realized had often been missing from her newspaper column as she'd raced to review the flavors of the food and ambiance of a restaurant. Story could add its own savory and sweet aspects, she was learning again.

"What story shall we tell your dad with food tonight?" Bullet ignored everything she had to say as he trotted over to his bed and began to bury his bone in slobber. She leaned against the counter and peeled a couple of mandarins for herself, her craving for all things citrus having gone through the roof.

It was a form of rebirth for Cass, this new manuscript, and every renewal required old layers to be shed. She was filled with anticipation about how her new writing self would appear to others. Before she'd mostly written for the readers. Now she wrote for them, but also for herself. And she hoped that combination would reach into people's hearts, because the writing of it thrilled her, and it made her realize she could write anywhere. With a smile she daydreamed about her new writing room in the house Adam was building for them. Here on this land was where she wanted to write.

So, scared or not, Cass reveled in the joy of her awakened creativity, her newfound sense of peace and home and found a new Thai curry recipe for a celebrational dinner. One with plenty of layers to entice Adam's kisses, to lure him further into her cave of love.

Chapter Thirty-Four

"Holy candy bars!" Lily yelled! She held Turner's hand in one of hers and the other waved the spring issue of *Travel Oregon*. "You're famous! We have a famous author right here at Brockman Farms. Where's a pen? I need an autograph. I bought all the copies the store had."

Turner set the wine box down on the table and Adam was surprised when magazines spilled from it. Lily gave Turner a smacking kiss before he left again.

"Be right back with the real drinks," he called.

"I'll help." Drake jogged after him. Cassandra's good friend Grant and his husband, Drake, were visiting from San Francisco.

They were at the main house for a family dinner-planning session for the opening of the café in two weeks. The first public barn dinner wouldn't happen for months due to weather and because starting both at the same time would be insane. Better to get their feet wet with the café first. For now, they were using the barn for family dinners and small local events for test purposes.

Lily had built a gorgeous café. Press releases had been sent out, staff had been trained and the menu was set, almost. Miranda and Katie were besides themselves with excitement and nerves. Well, Katie wasn't nervous. She sailed through life as if it were meant to be, ever since she'd walked out on T.D. hand in hand with Javier. *Love can do that to a person.* Cass' hand sat in his and he squeezed it. She grinned at him and let go to grab a copy.

Adam hadn't been much involved in the planning for any of it, unless he counted taste testing, which he showed up for whenever he could. And tonight was one final sampling of all the items on the menu and giving feedback since Miranda couldn't stop tweaking and fiddling. *Delicious* was the only feedback Adam had. Everything they'd been making over the last few months was going to be a hit. It would take intense focus to get work done and not hang out at the café all the time, begging for handouts.

"It's only a teaser paragraph. Teeny, almost invisible," Cass said, but excitement painted her face. "I've had more famous articles and essays published over the years." *How did I get so lucky?* He only wondered about a thousand times a day. *Super smart, talented, sexy as hell, bossy, kind, silly, proud.* His beauty was all these things and more. Her fingers shook as she paged through the magazine. Nervous was one emotion she didn't show often, and he wondered what it was about this "teeny" publication, as she called it, that had her shaking.

"Oh, they used the photograph I sent in. Miranda, it's one of yours."

"It's a perfect shot," Grant said, holding his own copy. "Illustrates how quaint and breathtaking this place is. Fanciful, mystical, secluded gem. Like walking into the Shire or eighteenth-century Scottish Highlands."

Grant had called it quaint when he'd first arrived and Adam had bristled, thinking they were mocking his farm. But as they'd all spent more time together this past weekend, he got it. Grant adored it here. And he had an extremely dramatic way with words. It probably did great things for his job as Arts & Theater Editor at the same newspaper Cass used to work for.

Normally Adam didn't give two squats about anyone else's opinion of this beautiful place and he was not a jealous person by nature at all. But Grant being Cass' best friend from the paper and urging Cass to come back... It wasn't jealousy that stirred like a restless stallion in his gut, or at least not of Grant.

Miranda, sweaty, aproned, hair piled on top of her head, flopped down on the bench next to Cass. "Look at us! I can't believe I took that photo. But the words..." She paused in reading and when she glanced up, her eyes were wet. "It's perfect. It's beautiful. It's exactly how I think of our café, 'Brilliant, unique, welcoming...with food that will blow your mind and warm your heart with lifelong memories.' I love it! You have such a way with words, Cass."

"And what about the proposal you sent out, to your old boss? Did he bite? What did he think?" Lily asked. Adam hadn't asked. He knew she'd sent a few. She was writing every day and talking up new ideas at night in the kitchen with him while she claimed more of his soul with her cooking.

"Jack loved it," Grant said "Haven't seen him that quiet ever. And, hold your horses, he actually cracked a smile when he was reading it. I thought he was going to shed a tear."

"No way." Cassandra laughed and shook her head. She winked at Adam and gave him her special secret smile, a knowing warm kiss of all the stories their bodies had been telling each other under the covers, on the kitchen counter, in that glorious shower as she called it. Even tucked into the bed in his Airstream, dark and cozy and mysterious, like their love at times. *And heated.* He burned for her always and she ached for him as much. *Two hearts connected.*

Next week would be three months since he'd brought her back with him. They'd started the new year together under clear, starlit skies over a frozen landscape. They'd been buried in their own bubble during that time, of discovery and lust, wanting and needing, taking and giving. *Love, dreaming.*

As much as it hurt to imagine, he knew they'd have to come out of that bubble at some point, and back into the rest of the world. She was going to be a sought-after author again, as she should be. Her old boss, *anyone* would be an idiot not to want her. And what did she want? He could only dream it would be him, but if she had the chance to go back to San Francisco?

Haunting fingers squeezed his chest.

"Trust me, I almost got a picture, but it had vanished by the time I got my phone out. You're going to get your old job back. Mark my words. Expect a call any day. You know I'm always right."

Bursting that bubble felt a whole lot different than he anticipated. Even surrounded by her beauty, by his family, it choked him. Maybe it was all a mirage. *Too good to be true.*

He stayed quiet and took it all in. Listening to her excitement over getting her writing mojo back was awesome, but it prodded open that old wound buried deep. It turned out he couldn't bury it deep enough. Even though she hadn't said it, he felt her love. Didn't he? It was the live thread beating between them. But could love win out over her career desires? Her passion, she'd called it. He couldn't keep her from it.

Ever since they'd been together, he'd known she wanted to get her career back. It was the first thing she'd mentioned when he asked her what her dreams were. It was no secret. But he'd been ignoring what that meant if she actually did. It wasn't like him to ignore issues. But he choked on his fear of what would happen if she decided she didn't want to stay. Because he knew he couldn't withstand her leaving again.

Chapter Thirty-Five

"Have you seen Cass?" Adam had finally showered off the muck of the day and made his way to the café. Cass wasn't at the cottage when he got there, which was odd. Even though she didn't sleep much during them, afternoon naps were still her jam, long lazy warm ones to rest her tired body. It was also still his favorite time of day, to climb in with her and explore that luscious naked body of hers. Or maybe mornings were his favorite, when the pink sun crested over the trees and she was needy. And the woman put a whole new meaning into *shower*.

He'd designed an enormous one along with a huge soaking tub for their master bedroom. He rubbed his hands together. The chill in the air had taken on a different tone, no longer the bitter windy days. It was still cold, but things were melting. *Finally*.

"Don't you dare set another foot inside this kitchen, Adam Brockman," his mother scolded. "I just mopped for the day." Yep, mud was everywhere, all over the farm, molded into every crack and crevice, stuck in all the tires, and even though he'd hosed it off, his boots were covered in it again from the walk over. Annoying as it was, he took it as a good sign. Spring was here. And spring on a farm was beautiful. Spring meant mud puddles, for sure, but it also meant seedlings sprouting, longer sunlit days, babies. *Lots and lots of babies.*

If Cass wasn't napping at the cottage, he knew where to find her—either the main house or café. She didn't so much work for them as hang out and get the scoop. None of them would let her help anyway unless it was in the form of eating their food and sharing her opinions. She was all too happy to oblige. Her appetite rivaled her desire for naps these days by a wide margin. And his grin turned smug when he thought of her sexual appetite. Adam had no complaints whatsoever. He was a lucky, lucky man.

He took the mop bucket from his mother to toss out the water. Miranda was there too when he handed it back. "Oh my God! Isn't it amazing and exciting? We're so happy for Cass! A book contract, I can't believe it!"

"I can't believe her editor and the publisher are in a battle for her manuscript." Lily was sneaking a tart out of the commercial fridge. "I mean a book sounds amazing, but to have her old title back at the paper, an entire year's worth of a new feature column already written? How does she choose?"

"What?" Adam could barely make sense of their words over the hammering in his heart.

"She didn't tell you yet?" His mom tilted her head. He'd been nearly waist-deep in mud all day fixing one of the old fences on the far reaches of the farm. She wouldn't have known where he was, but she might have called. He grabbed his cell phone from his shirt pocket, but there were no new messages.

"She raced over here with the news. Didn't she tell you first? Sailed out in a frenzy saying something about needing to go to San Francisco."

'Needing to go.' The hammering turned to thunder in his ears.

"Oh, honey, go find her, let her share her joy with you and tell you all about it," Katie said. But all joy was pounded out of his heart at the idea of Cass returning to San Francisco.

* * * *

The cottage was empty again when he returned. He took off toward the barns, Bullet racing by his side. Cass belonged to Bullet as much as she belonged to Adam. Or she had. He knew they belonged together, here on Brockman land. *Have I been wrong?* His mind raced with misinterpretations, with choices, with the heartbreak of her leaving again, this time for good. He'd sworn he'd never make her chose between him and her career and he kept his promises. A man was no kind of good man if he didn't. One more lesson he'd learned from Javier. But if she left, she'd take his heart with her and his life would be snuffed out. No more could he renege on his promises than go back to gray from the technicolor she'd painted through his life.

The barn was quiet this time of day, with no Cassandra there, either. Their house? Would she have gone up there for any reason? The damn thing wasn't even finished yet. Fuck, he'd been taking his time getting their house built, getting a solid plan built for them. Adam had lingered too long in their dreamy bubble, but as he crested the hill and saw their house in the distance, the weight of eschewing his responsibilities slammed into him.

The whole thing still needed siding, floors. The bathrooms weren't finished. They were waiting for custom kitchen cabinets. *Her dream kitchen exactly how she wanted it.* He'd let her design it. Who the hell was supposed to use it now that she was leaving? Bullet? He should have been up here through the nights, helping get shit done, helping to make her feel secure. Making sure she knew that he was committed.

"Cassandra!" he yelled. "Cass! Are you here?" In all his frustration, one thing was clear. He hadn't done enough to show her that when he said he wanted a lifetime with her, he meant it. And there was only one thing to do to make things right—prove to her that no matter where she was, he wanted to be with her. Even if it meant giving all this up, the land, the farm, their house, his horses. He'd find a way to make it all work. He had to. She was his heartbeat and he had to believe she was his.

Out of breath, he ran around the house and barged into his trailer, musty in its closed-up state. They'd only spent a handful of hours here since they'd returned. He'd checked in every week to make sure the hiding place he'd chosen for the ring he'd gotten was still safe and secure. *The ring.* He'd have to wait to give it to her now, or it might come across as a begging type of engagement instead of her being his everything type of engagement.

Hell, maybe she wouldn't want to get married now. Could he do that, be with her without being married? His eyes were wide fucking open now. *Anything.* He'd do anything for her.

He tossed clothes into his large duffle bag, paying no attention to what he was grabbing or how it was folded.

"Adam! Adam!" Yelling dragged him back from crazy town. She stood before him, tugging on his arm. Bullet sat by her side, tongue hanging out, leaning his weight into both of them.

Adam grabbed her to him and gasped. "Cass!" He roamed his hands all over her to make sure she was real while he caught his breath. "Thank fuck. You didn't leave without me. I'm coming with you if you'll have me. You'll have to show me around, be patient while I adapt to city life, but I'll go anywhere you want, be anywhere you want." He kissed her like his life depended on it, most likely because it fucking did.

Chapter Thirty-Six

Swept up in his ravaging kiss, Cass indulged for a few moments, hours — who knew how long — until his words and his frantic demeanor registered in her brain and she pulled away. The sun was hanging in the sky longer and longer as they crept out of winter, but it was still dark in here. As her eyes adjusted to what was before her, her brain felt like mush. *What the heck is he doing?*

"You're packing?" *More like freaking out.* But the suitcase and piles of clothes dragged from his drawers hinted at what was happening. "Where are you going?"

"With you."

She huffed out a confused laugh and pushed him down to sitting on the bed because the poor man was half out of his mind and exhausted. When she stepped between his legs, he grasped her hips. Cass took his face in her hands. "Would you like to tell me where I'm going? Where *we're* going?" She flung out her hand to the mess of half-packed clothes.

"Back to San Francisco for your career, your book deal so you don't have to choose. I love you. I want to go with you if you'll have me." *What?* Silly man, what was he thinking? They already had each other. Then he exploded her world with his vulnerability. "I know it might be too soon for you to say you love me. I'll wait for as long as you need. But I don't know if I'll survive if you leave me again and I can't expect you to give up your career. So I'll go with you." Then he gently rested his forehead on her belly and released a long, ragged breath, like a panicked drowning man holding on to his last thread of hope.

Oh, Lordy. Cass pulled his head up and pushed him onto the bed. She kicked off her boots and climbed over him so she was straddling his body. "First of all, honey" —Cass took one of his hands and rested it on her heart—"I promise never to leave you again. It's obvious I haven't done a great job of making you believe how much I love you and love it here. I'm so sorry. Is that why you've been awfully quiet the last few days?" She watched the truth pass over his features.

"I'm not going to San Francisco." She shook her head. "Neither of us are, at least not to move there. I need to go for a visit soon because people want my book and I have contracts to read."

"Yeah." He ran his hands up her thighs. "I heard, beautiful." When the truth of everything he'd said, of what he was willing to do, all he was willing to sacrifice hit her, it was almost too much for Cass to handle.

"You were going to leave all this behind for me?" Her words were barely a whisper through her tears. She rested her hands on his solid biceps and took comfort in the depth of his love for her.

"I'd do anything for you, darlin'," he swore.

"Adam Brockman, do you know how much I love you? My love for you is wider than the galaxy and all the stars in the sky and all the glitter everywhere."

His heart warmed, and he gently rolled them over to their sides so they faced each other. He carefully dragged her leg over his and did his sexy move that connected them tight in all the right places, only a bit different now, thanks to her baby belly. "You love me?"

Bullet barked and jumped onto the end of the bed before he flopped his butt up and front down like her love for Adam was something to play about. They both burst out laughing.

"Honey, I fell in love with you under the stars on our first walk, out on this beautiful field when you showed me where you wanted to build your house, when you came to San Francisco for me. I fall more in love every time I watch you care for your horses, with every hug you give me. My love for you grows every day. I'd like to fall in love with you into forever, if you'll have me. Right here or there." She gestured toward where their house was being built. "Your farm brought me back to life. You make me feel beloved every day."

"You love me." His eyes shone with happiness when he said it again and she giggled because he was so dang cute.

"Yes, Adam Brockman. I love you with all my heart." Then she put all that love into kissing him.

"My darlin'." Adam gazed at her. "You got some good news today."

"Yes!" she squealed, wide-eyed. "Who told you?"

"The ladies. All of them. They thought I knew already."

"I couldn't find you. I looked everywhere and when I stopped at the kitchen and they fed me one of their leek and goat cheese tarts, I spilled the beans. I was too excited to keep it in."

His huge smile told her he was happy for her, no matter who found out first. "What are you going to do, have you decided?"

She nodded.

"Well?" He tickled her side.

"Oh!" *Oh.* Her eyes got huge, almost as big as his.

He put his hand back on the side of her belly where he'd tickled. "Was that the munchkin?"

This time when she nodded, the tears rushed back in, not to be left out of any moment these days. "Baby Sweets has been kicking up a storm since this morning. I think he or she might have soccer player in their future."

"Mmm." He studied her belly with awe and love. "Or astronaut, or teacher, or nurse." She loved the way he envisioned their future, the future of their baby as a world of endless possibilities. "Can't wait to hold her."

"How do you know it's going to be a girl?"

"Just a feeling," he said, kissing her again. He was probably right. This man and his confidence were so fricking handsome and attractive. "So...my superstar writer?"

"I'll study the contracts, but I already know what my heart's telling me to do and I'm going to listen. I'm going to stay at this precious place called Brockman Farms, my new home, with my love." She ran her hands through his hair, a gesture he always leaned into. "And celebrate turning my essays into a book!"

Adam took her mouth in a soft kiss this time. His tenderness, the way he held her, would be her complete undoing. When he rolled away for a minute, she thought it was to get her tissues, but instead he held a small red velvet box in his hands.

Cass gasped. "I don't know whether to laugh or cry."

But her sexy farmer knew what to do. Adam tangled their fingers together, kissed her knuckles and said, "Cassandra Dorsey, will you be my starlight, my moon, my summer rainstorm and field of wildflowers? Will you be my love forever?"

"Yes, yes, yes," she said through all of it, through her tears, her laughter and her love.

Chapter Thirty-Seven

Cass had never seen a barn dressed up so prettily. Her ladies – Annabelle, Lily, Miranda, Katie, Elena, Roxanna, even her mother who'd flown in from Florida – had gone bonkers with the decorations. Chic, classy bonkers. Long wood tables were covered in gorgeous gray table runners, dotted with glitter. Vases of wild roses, anemones, poppies and flowing greenery added color, and short candles twinkled with light. White plates, rose and gray wine glasses and shiny silverware sat at each place setting. Above them were twice as many lights as normally graced the ceiling, and fairy lights draped from the old beams. Gorgeous spring flowers filled enormous silver buckets along the walls. The buffet was almost set up. Their friends Roxanna and Miguel had provided staff tonight so Miranda and Katie could enjoy the event as guests and not as proprietors.

A band played in one corner, while another corner housed the bar Adam and his brothers had built. At the end of the buffet sat another table full of presents.

A party fit for a princess, including the dress she'd found in San Francisco on a shopping trip with Annabelle, Miranda and Lily. Navy blue, off the shoulder, hugging over her belly and swaying to mid-ankle with a slit up the side, both beautiful and sexy. Tiny sparkly gems lined the fabric, curving over her collarbone and dipping between her breasts. Every inch of the dress tantalized and sculpted her large curves. Cass felt the glow from around her and within. Even her sore, tired back wasn't going to get in the way of the magic spell cast upon all of them tonight to celebrate love, although she might kick off her silver heels as soon as everyone sat down to dinner.

Adam stood, watching her from across the room with that same hooded sexy look that spoke volumes of erotic teasing to her body. Cass walked up and slipped her hand into his. "Mr. Brockman, may I have this dance?"

He set his glass down on the bar and smiled while leading her to the center of the barn. "Absolutely, Mrs. Brockman." Instead of facing her, he wrapped his arms around her from behind and swayed them around the dance floor, carefully, preciously. Her enormous belly made it impossible to dance like normal, but this was fabulous. His front pressed up against her back, his cheek resting against hers. Everyone faded into the sparkly night background. It was just the two of them and some mellow jazz.

"Have I told you how gorgeous you are, darlin'?"

She laughed. "Only about a hundred times."

He acted affronted. "I'm not that corny. It's probably only been eighty."

"Well, even if you haven't said it out loud, every look you give me burns with it."

"No." His head shook against hers. "My look says I can't wait to peel this gorgeous fucking dress off you tonight in our new bed, relish your skin, your curves, all your hot secret places and make love to you in our new home for the first time."

"What do you call what we did in that amazeballs shower a few hours ago?" They'd christened their finally finished, stunning new home in a perfect way, their new shower big enough for a party, rain shower head and side sprays and a bench. Mmm, that bench was sturdy too. They'd tested it. She couldn't wait to try out the tub with him, but that would have to wait until after the baby came. If she could even get into the thing right now, there was absolutely no way she'd be able to get out.

"Fantastic." He nibbled her ear. "That's what I call it. Do you know how happy I am? I thought I was happy before you walked into my vision, but I was merely content. Content is a lonely, forgotten planet. You flung me into the atmosphere to fly free without gravity."

"You know you're the real bard in this family," she said and smiled as he pressed up tighter against her. She loved giving him compliments, cheering him on, loving him.

Other couples took to the dance floor around them and slowly the song came to an end. The scene settled back in around her. "Anyone hungry?" Lily yelled. Laughter ruffled through the crowd. This group was always hungry.

"How do you like your party, Cassandra?" he asked. Adam took her hand and twirled her out, then led her to the head of the table where their chairs sat next to each other.

"I couldn't have asked for anything better."

"And unique," he added. "This is the first combination baby shower and wedding I've ever been to."

The ceremony had finished an hour ago, quiet and sweet, on their hill with the sun setting over the ocean. They'd all walked back to the barn on a perfect, warm, clear night, as the stars began to twinkle, for the after celebration. "I love it." Cass kissed his hand and rested them next to each other on the table. "Fits us perfectly, don't you think, doing things in our own wacky way."

He flipped their hands so they were intertwined. "Unpredictable is amazing."

The 'Caribbean meets Mexican meets all manner of bread' theme of the dinner was one hundred percent focused on Cassandra's cravings lately, jerk chicken and smoked pork shoulder with salsas and crunchy salads, and bread, always bread.

The music bounced and glittered off the lights to create a 3D effect. She could hear the songs through the lights, elegant and seductive. After dinner they laughed and joked at the presents everyone had brought them. From baby diapers and sleep machines to new cookbooks featuring women chefs from around the world. Not to be left out, Adam's brothers had teased him with a *Sex for Dummies* book, which Adam took in good fun with a smirk on his face and a secret hand-squeeze for Cass. Her man did not need a book, but they might have fun laughing at some of the descriptions. Cassandra floated above all of it, basking in the night's shimmery glow.

Aside from one teeny tiny issue.

"Are we diving into that caramel layer cake now or what?" Lily asked. She strolled around the tables and poured coffee and more wine for everyone.

Cass snuggled in as much as she could to Adam and whispered in his ear. His smile turned from casual and warm to open-mouthed surprise to pure excitement. "Really?" he said to her and immediately put his hand on her belly.

When she nodded, he turned to their friends and family and yelled, "Save us some dessert. Hospital, here we come. We're having a baby!"

* * * *

"How are you feeling?" Adam asked brushing a kiss over the baby's head who slept on Cass' chest, nose pressed into her mama's neck. He kissed his wife next. *My wife and my baby. Thank fuck they're all right. I'm the luckiest man alive.* Cass' eyes fluttered and she yawned.

"Tired. Amazing."

Color had returned to her cheeks, and she glowed, even after everything she'd been through. A blood transfusion and some sleep had helped.

He'd been here watching them and hadn't left their sides the entire time. Not when his brave darlin' pushed their baby into the world. Not when the spectacular moment shot from wonderful happy occasion to emergency in a matter of minutes, and not now when Cass finally got to hold her baby. He'd stand vigil over them forever. It was a good thing his heart had started back up. She had a habit of scaring the life out of him.

Cass grabbed his hand. "Look at her cheeks. Our little chipmunk."

Adam let go the strangled breath he'd been holding for the last few hours since Willa May Brockman had made her debut. The rush of Willa's birth had been momentarily eclipsed by Cass losing consciousness and her body trying to bleed out, the worst thing he'd ever witnessed.

"And her fuzzy hair." Adam peeked under the soft baby hat Miranda had tucked into Cass' bag. "She's beautiful."

"She's impatient. Two weeks early and we barely made it to the hospital in time." Cass gave a soft gentle laugh. "Guess she didn't want to miss out on the party."

"She *is* the party." He nuzzled his kiss gently into the other side of Cass' neck and placed his hand over hers resting on Willa.

"You okay, honey?" she whispered in her soft soothing tone.

It took him a few minutes to answer through the tears. "Yeah," he said finally, and met her gaze. "Grateful. So damn grateful. I didn't know my heart could get any bigger, but it's exploding."

"I love you, too," she said. And he let those words sooth the hollows of fear lingering in his gut.

"Are our goofballs still out there?" Everyone had followed them to the hospital, his family, hers. The doctors had only let Katie in to hold Willa for now. But his baby girl was lucky. She had an overflowing hospital waiting room of family and friends to get to know.

"I sent them all home a while ago when everything settled down. It's the middle of the night, but they said they'd be back in the morning and I have no doubt it's true."

Cass grew serious. "I hope they bring donuts."

Adam chuckled and relaxed into his chair. "Now I know you're feeling better." He reached for the box behind him. "I don't have donuts, but I do have this." He opened it to show her slices of the caramel layer cake they'd missed out on from their party and watched her smile and her eyes grow. Then they snuggled in while he fed her cake and they marveled over their own tiny bit of magic.

Epilogue

The world settled quietly around him, aside from the muffled squish of Gracie's hooves through the snow as Adam walked her across the white field. Above him the sky was white with heavy clouds blocking the sun, and stretched out all around him, the land was blanketed in snow. His farm was gorgeous in winter. Big fluffy flakes floated down around him and Willa who was tucked cozily into the baby carrier strapped to his chest. Facing out, she squealed and kicked every time a flake drifted into her tiny palms.

"Yeah, possum, snow," he said, swishing some of the white fluff off Gracie's mane.

"So, so, so," his girl chanted with her entire precious body. She'd brought so much into their lives already in only seven months. Adam was learning how to be a better man every day with her. She might have taken their sleep away, but she'd opened their hearts further to so much joy, so much warmth and laughter and awe and love. She'd even given him a new appreciation for winter. Her delight in everything around her had opened his eyes to a new way of viewing everything, including his land, his family, his life.

With the sun setting, it was time to get Gracie back. Plus, he and his girl had a party to get to. Patiently, Willa watched while he led Gracie into her stall and set the saddle back on its rack. She 'helped' him brush the mare down, give her food and water and cover her with the blanket, but when it was time to go, she screeched and grabbed Gracie's mane, trying to bury her face in the horse's neck.

"Come on, let's go see your mama."

Willa kicked out and screeched, "Ma ma ma ma ma!" Gracie had a special place in his girl's heart, but Cass was Willa's favorite person. And Adam absolutely understood why. Cassandra was his favorite person too, right beside Willa. They were covered in a white dusting by the time they made it to the main house for Christmas Eve dinner. The place was crawling with people as everyone got ready for the feast. His smile turned soft and knowing when Cass' gaze caught his across the café. She had her arm around his mother. Cruz and Miranda were heaping piles of food onto platters and Miguel set the long tables with his son Juan Carlos. Roxanna laughed at something Jake's girlfriend had said while her kids helped set the food on the tables.

There were too many of them to eat in the kitchen or dining room. Besides, it felt right to use the café for their celebration tonight. *Full of friends and family.* Lily swept right over and unbuckled Willa from the baby carrier, tossing her baby hat and coat on the heater by the door.

"My snuggle bunny." She hugged the baby and sneaked tickles at her side, which had his girl laughing and kicking again. "Wait till you see what I have for you." Lily whisked her away to the dessert table covered in cookies and sweet rolls and cakes. He should amend his earlier thought that Cass was Willa's favorite. Lily often soared past them all into first place. His girl had a sweet tooth, and her auntie was happy to indulge her. Grant and Turner met Lily at the dessert table and tried to get Willa's attention, but even with their kisses and Turner's new beard that Willa loved, she was laser focused on the sweet bun Lily had given her.

When it was time for dinner, Javier tucked her right onto his lap and Willa sat quietly studying the man in awe while he fed her. He had her under his spell. He was the only one she was patient and contemplative for. And when she started to fall asleep while eating, Annabelle took her and stood, swaying her into slumber. Next to Adam, his wife rested her head on his shoulder and sighed with happiness. "Magic, isn't it?" she whispered.

Love was all around him, in so many more ways than he ever imagined possible. He and Cass were surrounded by it and more importantly, Willa was. She'd grow up knowing she was fiercely wanted, fiercely loved.

Adam hadn't even realized he'd been lacking anything until Cass had shown up in his life. He'd been limited in his expectations of what life had for him. Now he lived surrounded by it, by passion and creativity and friendship and love, brighter than all the stars in the sky. And now he'd work every day to teach his girl what Cassandra had taught him, that love was limitless. That love in all its forms could last forever.

Want to see more from this author? Here's a taster for you to enjoy!

Rescue Me: Igniting Love
Sara Ohlin

Excerpt

"Penny, I'm here!" Katie shouted into the seemingly empty penthouse apartment twenty-five floors in the sky. She lugged in her bags overflowing with groceries. "Penny?" There were several boxes, some open, strewn across the entry hallway, and packaging popcorn left a trail toward Penny's office.

It wasn't uncommon for Katie's clients to be gone when she arrived. As a personal chef, she mostly cooked alone. But Penny Jager, successful sex therapist-turned-author, worked from her home, with its stunning view into Corvallis. Today, however, clouds hovered around the building, blanketing the town below, thickheaded and still, like a pouty six-year-old determined to wear her pajamas to school. The lack of scenery outside the floor-to-ceiling windows unbalanced Katie. *Surreal to be up so high and not see anything but puffs of white.*

"Be out in a minute!" Penny yelled from her office. "Sorry for the mess!"

I wonder if those clouds are as stubborn as my six-year old? It sure was a relief not to have to be at a job exactly on time. As a widow and a mom of three girls, Katie was never on time. She had barely dropped her youngest, Cece, off at the elementary school this morning before the bell rang. One more tardy and she'd be getting the dreaded note home about how attendance matters. *Gah! And it's only October.*

Katie unloaded food and supplies and jotted down her task list. First, she checked the coffee — nearly empty. She ground beans and brewed a fresh pot for Penny who mainlined caffeine during the day. Next, Katie boiled water for the baked pasta she'd pair with meatballs and homemade pomodoro sauce.

She measured breadcrumbs and chopped fresh parsley. The repetition, the way Katie coordinated everything, brought her a level of comfort and energized her. *Or it used to.* She glanced up to the still-shrouded view. *Out of balance, and not just from the clouds. More than out of balance. Needy, wanting.*

She used her hands to mix the ingredients together then rolled them into meatballs and placed them on a plate to chill in the refrigerator. "It's not your fault, guys," she said to the food. Cooking wasn't the problem. She still loved making food. It was just that, lately, her job, her *life* felt —

"Oh, thank God you're here. I'm starving! We're socked in like a cock in a too tight condom, I imagine. And look at you talking to balls." Penny sailed in, barefoot and wearing what looked like a long fuchsia caftan over lounge-type pants.

Katie wouldn't tell Cece that some people did get to wear their pajamas all day. Penny was nothing if not dramatic and blunt, both of which served her well in her profession. Luckily for Katie, she was also kind, full of compassion and had offered friendship as well as a paycheck in exchange for Katie's meals. She was Katie's favorite client.

Penny grabbed the enormous twelve-cup pot. "Coffee, love?" She grabbed a mug for Katie. "And please tell me you're making those chocolate chip muffins this morning."

"Better," Katie said. "I made them at home." She unwrapped a huge muffin and plated it for Penny. "Might still be warm."

"Heaven." Penny sighed after swallowing a bite. "Tempt me with the rest of the week's menu."

"Steak salad with farfalle, spicy chicken for tacos and I'm not telling you any more." Penny was also her favorite client because she let Katie surprise her each week. Several of Katie's clients ordered the exact same meals. Every time.

"Mmm-hmm, what's got you sighing and lamenting over balls? Or is it the lack of balls in your life?" Penny's laugh was full and deep, like a jazzy lounge singer in a smoky bar.

Katie's face heated. "Hah! I was thinking how much I enjoy cooking for you because I get to interact with you."

"And have me drool over your creations."

"That doesn't hurt either." Once the cans of tomatoes were open, she chopped onions. "I never see the rest of my clients. After John died, when I started personal cheffing, the solitude wasn't a problem. I looked forward to it, for the calm compared to the rest of my life and because I was barely keeping my head above water. I didn't have time to get bored. Things were crazy busy, as they are now."

"I bet, with three young divas at home."

Katie laughed. Her daughters *were* divas. One teenage angsty diva, one serene know-it-all middle-kid diva and one loud drama-queen-six-year-old-going-on-twenty-six diva. "But now, I notice empty spaces.

Does that make sense? I don't mean to sound ungrateful. But I want connection, more adults in my life. I want to share my love of food and cooking with people, not just cook by myself all the time."

"You're lonely. How could you not be? You're raising three girls on your own, you work your butt off as a mom and business owner and you have so much to give the world. Bet you're feeling lonely in the bedroom, too."

"Oh no you don't." Katie raised her hand. "I'm not one of your patients."

"You're my friend. And you don't have to be one of my patients for me to see you're in a sexual desert."

"What, parched? Searching for my oasis?" Katie smirked.

"Exactly. Needy, unfulfilled. Wanting and enjoying a healthy sex life is normal, Katie. How long has it been?"

She didn't hide her sigh. *Way too long.* She did miss sex lately. Jeez, was it written on her face or did Penny have a *sex* sense? "Since John died."

"Five years? That's no desert—that's Mars!"

"Calm down." *Should I laugh or cry?* "When should I have found the time, running my three divas to their activities, keeping them from killing each other, saving the house from my brother's ridiculous decision to toss a puppy into the mix, working full-time, scheduling one more stupid car maintenance appointment?"

"Single parents date, Katie. You just have to make the effort. Figure out what you want. There are such things as babysitters. Mmm. Do you want to find someone again? Enjoy sex again?"

Yes, and yes, please. Too choked up all of a sudden to voice the words, she nodded. She wanted both. Hot oil from the sautéing onions zapped her hand when Katie stirred the garlic in. "Ouch!" she yelped and ran her hand under cold water.

"That's a sign to take a break. Come with me. Wouldn't you know these boxes arrived today of all days."

Katie turned off the burner and followed Penny down the hall.

"We might need some whiskey in our coffee to have this discussion," Penny mumbled to herself. "My agent seems to have a fortuitous sense of humor."

Katie stepped into Penny's bright office. Boxes similar to those in the entryway sat open with packaging strewn over the floor. Brightly colored items shaped like rods o...*oh!*

"A company called Love Handle wants me to review their new products."

"*Sex toys?*" Katie asked.

"Honey, people don't come to me for tax help. They want to enjoy life, find pleasure in the bedroom again. Or on the dining room table or in the sauna. With or without a partner." Penny calmed her laughter before taking a sip of coffee.

Katie picked up a silver dildo bigger than any real cock she'd ever seen. "'Lonely Lady's Friend.' It's apropos, but the name certainly doesn't make me feel better."

"That's just it. It *might* make you feel a whole lot better. Look, there's something for everyone's tastes. Pun intended. Musical themes like The Slow Jam, mmm-hmm. Or A Day's Hard Night. How about a fantasy line to tickle your fancy? A bit expected calling this one Unicorn, but look at the rainbow ribbed feel."

Penny was having way too much fun with this.

"And good Lord, even techies need their toys — The Code Hacker. Oh! Here's the box for you — food themes. Delicious."

"God, don't tell me they're all different sausage names?" Katie couldn't help her grin.

"Oh, no, much cleverer than that." Penny wiped the tears of laughter from her eyes. "Oh, I do love my job." She handed her a shiny gold vibrator. "Butter Finger."

Katie's neck was warm and she knew it bloomed bright red.

"Tell you what," Penny said. "As much as I do enjoy a healthy sex life, there's no way I can test all of these products myself. I think you should pick a few sexy toys and give them a go. Then report back."

"No way. I can't just try out a" — Katie held up what looked like a sparkly pink set of silicone beads connected on a chain — "on command."

Even Penny blushed. She took that one out of Katie's hands. "We should start you on some more familiar play. I'll keep the butt toys for later."

Butt toys? Katie buried her face in her hands, which only made Penny laugh harder. "I'm going to need an instruction manual for these tools."

"Ooo, good one — you need to handle a man's tool all right."

Penny's teasing and innuendos could make anyone laugh, Katie included.

"You're suggesting I need to spearhead my own research," Katie said. Maybe she could get the hang of this.

"Exactly, find someone to shuck your oyster."

"Oh! Stop!" Katie said, choking on her own laughter. "Too far."

"Okay…" Penny got more serious. "I think you do need more than toys. You need emotions and desire.

Your assignment is to go out at least once before I see you next week. Schedule a blind date. Head out to a fun bar for girls' night. Sign up for online dating. Talk to a hot guy. Flirt your cute butt off. Anything for adults. Leave all your responsibilities at home and start taking care of your health. Practice, practice, practice."

Home of Erotic Romance

Sign up for our newsletter and find out about all our romance book releases, eBook sales and promotions, sneak peeks and FREE romance books!

About the Author

Sara Ohlin has lived all over the United States, but her heart keeps getting pulled back to the Pacific Northwest where it belongs. For years she has been writing creative non-fiction and memoir and feels that writing helps her make sense of this crazy world. She devours books and can often be found shushing her two hilarious kids so that she can finish reading. When she isn't reading or writing, she'll most likely be in the kitchen cooking up something scrumptious, a French macaron, shrimp scampi, a fun date-night-in dinner with her sexy husband, or perhaps her next love story.

Sara loves to hear from readers. You can find her contact information, website details and author profile page at https://www.totallybound.com